·LOT'S WIFE·

Tom Wakefield

SERPENT'S
TAIL

BRITISH LIBRARY CATALOGUING
IN PUBLICATION DATA

Wakefield, Tom
Lot's Wife
I.Title
823'.914[F]
ISBN 1-85242-152-5

First published 1989 by
Serpent's Tail, 4 Blackstock Mews, London N4
Copyright © 1989 by Tom Wakefield

Typeset in 10/13pt Ehrhardt by Selectmove Ltd.

Printed in Denmark by
Nørhaven A/S, Viborg, Denmark

Clinical diagnoses are important, since they give the doctor a certain orientation; but they do not help the patient. The crucial thing is the story. For it alone shows the human background and the human suffering.

Memories, Dreams, Reflections
C.G. Jung

For – In Memoriam
Esther Wakefield, Thomas Collie and J.G. Farrell

·LOT'S WIFE·

CHAPTER

1

'One for sorrow.' Henry Checket sighed and scanned the lawn.

'Ah, thank God for that – two for joy.' He smiled as two more magpies glided past like World War II Nazi dive-bombers. 'Three for a girl, and four for a boy.'

From his small bedroom he looked out into a garden whose size, space and natural grandeur only served to emphasise the meanness of his own surroundings. He had a single bed now covered with a pink candlewick bedspread, a small table, and a loom chair that creaked. He had only to breathe heavily and the damned chair would sigh. A steel wardrobe held his clothes, a chest of drawers his papers. Even this meagre furnishing left little space for movement inside the room.

Outside, there was a lot of space to look out upon. At seventy-eight years he felt that he could only travel and explore with his mind. His body could not carry him any great distance. Only his grasshopper mind could offer him any transport.

It was the first of October and the lawns of the garden were green and well-trimmed. Tubs of pink and blue hydrangeas stood on the stone flags surrounding the lily pond. The flower beds beyond held the remnants of some late-flowering yellow roses but these were put to shame by great clumps of pale lilac-coloured Michaelmas daisies and bushes of red and deep purple flowering fuchsia.

The four magpies seemed to have a shared intent. They were destroying something. Through the open window he could hear the dying squeaks of some creature. Henry did not hear Mrs Fairhurst enter his room. This was not surprising as she had not knocked.

'Well, well, well. You're still here, Mr Checket. We can't have that, Mr Checket, can we? Glad to see that you are dressed. It's one o'clock. You've missed your morning coffee. The others were wondering where you were. We can't have that. We can't have you moping in your room on a lovely day like this, can we? Do you know what day it is?' Mrs Fairhurst spoke from somewhere behind his left shoulder. He did not turn to answer, but said:

'Funny birds, magpies, nasty creatures. Predatory.'

'It's Wednesday, Mr Checket.'

'They eat the eggs, even the young, of other birds. Some say they even eat the young of their own species.'

'I said it's Wednesday today, Mr Checket.' Mrs Fairhurst spoke as though Henry were deaf when his hearing was quite perfect.

'Ah, did you? You are alone. You said "we". I thought you were with someone.'

'Naughty boy, you did hear me. I can expect you down, then?'

'Mmm – mmm.'

Mrs Fairhurst left the room shaking her head. Henry Checket had been at Restmore Haven for just over seven months and Mrs Fairhurst felt quite exasperated by him. But she would not give up. She would not let him retreat into that private world which often heralded senile dementia for the elderly. As she stepped lightly and carefully down the stairs she was given hope by the recollection of her own words at the interview for the position of officer-in-charge of Restmore.

'The elderly are part of the community – some of them because of the past or the dismal present wish to retreat into a world which is less challenging. Withdrawn behaviour of this kind is often an indicator of mental, physical, intellectual and emotional decline. I will do my utmost not to let this happen. Restmore will be a place to live, not to die.'

Mrs Fairhurst had been thrilled by the heroic nature of her own vision. She ran a progressive home for the forty or so residents. She worked extremely hard and her energy and enthusiasm never waned. She smiled a good deal and still managed to be efficient. Visitors to the home were always full of praise and awe. 'I don't know how you do it, Mrs Fairhurst, I really don't.' Mrs Fairhurst always brushed such compliments aside with modest shrugs. In herself, she glowed. This was her world, her order. The nature of her idealism and compassion was bounded by her own assumptions. She decided what was good for her and for them.

The elderly inhabitants of Restmore were rarely seen sitting around. Even television was only allowed three evenings a week. Mrs Fairhurst believed in activities. It was almost as though her inmates had returned to infants' school, except that choice was not in abundance and that Mrs Fairhurst often referred to many of the activities as therapy.

As a result of a weekend course in social dynamics (attended during her one weekend off the previous month) Mrs Fairhurst was now initiating a new activity which she was to run herself. Little posters had gone up to announce it and a group of twelve had been gleaned from the residents. There was little choice for them but to attend. Mrs Fairhurst's schooling was compulsory. Within ten minutes the first 'Reminiscence Therapy Session' was about to commence.

Mrs Fairhurst sat and smiled and looked at the chairs around her. The activity had a double object. She was welcoming her students and checking on the numbers. One was missing – but oh – there was Mr Checket taking his seat at the window. He sat with his back to the light and his face was obscured by shadow.

'Close the doors – would you, Mrs Tate – yes, as you go out. Thank you.' Mrs Fairhurst then lapsed naturally into her use of the collective. 'Now, all nice and comfy, are we?' She did not pause to give her clients a chance to say they were not. 'Yes, of course, we are. Now, can anyone tell me what this is?' Mrs Fairhurst held up a gruesome looking doll which had somehow lost its left leg and right arm. It had great bald patches on its head which might indicate that it had suffered some terrible nervous disorder. Her question was received in silence. It was quite clear to all the onlookers what the thing was – or what it had been.

'Now, Peggy – you know what it is, don't you?' Mrs Fairhurst's question directed at the small, elderly widow to her right was more of an order than a request. Peggy Thurston wanted to say: 'It's a doll – you silly cow,' but she answered quietly.

'It's a doll, Mrs Fairhurst. Like the ones we had in the old days.' Mrs Fairhurst placed the doll on the floor and then raised both her hands infected with delight. 'Give Mrs Thurston a clap. Come on, everyone, give Mrs Thurston a clap.' The audience dutifully obeyed.

'Do you know who that doll belonged to? Yes, it was me. It was my dolly. And I still have it. Why do I keep it? Well, I'll tell you why I keep that useless, old, raggedy broken-down doll.' Mrs Fairhurst did not pause to think what effect such words would have on her clients but rushed on – fascinated by her own histrionics.

'I have her near me because she brings back happy memories of when I was a girl. Oh, happy, happy times they were. She's called Nancy. And through all my difficult times – often when I've felt bowed with sorrow – I've always talked to her. Why do you think I do that?'

'Well, she can't answer back, can she?' said Mrs Thurston. There were a few cautionary titters from the others.

'No, that is not the reason, Mrs Thurston.' Mrs Fairhurst seized the doll by its single arm and held it aloft. 'Nancy is a love object.' Henry thought it looked a very dubious thing to love but kept silent.

Mrs Fairhurst licked her top lip and continued. 'When I look at my little Nancy I am always reminded of my dear mother.'

'Oh, was she handicapped?' Mrs Thurston asked innocently.

Don't interrupt any more, dear. We'll have time for questions later.'

Henry turned himself on the chair so that he could look at the view from the french windows. He did not wish to upset Mrs Fairhurst but the thought of giving her his undivided attention for fifteen minutes or more held little enchantment for him. In fact, he was sure that he would find it wearisome. Mrs Fairhurst's voice, even when she was at her most solicitous, had a harshness to it that he had always found most unattractive. He looked out at the garden and there was no movement. Even the magpies had stopped their foraging. He listened for sounds but heard only Mrs Fairhurst.

'When I was nine, no, I tell you all a lie. When I was eight and a half I was very unfortunate. I lost my father. Yes, my father passed on when I was only a child.' She paused and waited for a murmur of sympathy. None came and she quickened her pace. 'My mother was left a widow with two young children to bring up. That was myself and my elder brother Charles who was just fourteen. We kept a newsagents shop in Tottenham. It was a better class of person living in that area in those days. You know, I thought that my mother would close the shop. But no, not a bit of it, not my mother. It was as though my father's death had given extra petrol to her engine. Like me, she was always an active woman. With the insurance from my father's death she opened a tinned grocery section and increased the confectionary stock.' Mrs Fairhurst paused and smiled in a self-satisfied way. 'The shop was rarely empty. There was always someone on the other side of the counter.' At this point she raised her forefinger. 'But she didn't always sell . . . she gave.'

'It's a wonder she didn't go bust,' someone murmured.

'She gave support and she gave it lovingly and freely.' Mrs Fairhurst said this as though her mother was some kind of saintly analyst. 'But, of course, it left me alone for great periods of time. And that is why my mother gave me dear Nancy. "This is a special doll, my dear. Tell her your joys and sorrows as you would your own mother because mummy won't be around as much as she was." And now, when I want private comfort or sometimes even advice I still sometimes ask Nancy.' Mrs Fairhurst held the doll to her bosom and asked: 'Why do you think I do that?'

'As I said, she can't answer back.'

'No, no, no . . . Nancy is a love object. She is a reminder of my dear mother and my family.' Mrs Fairhurst brushed away a tear that had not appeared and let her narrative rest, much to the relief of most of the listeners.

'Now, I'm going to ask each one of you, in turn. I'm going to ask you to tell me about something which brings back memories and makes you feel happy.'

Most of those assembled just made up a reply. Three took an easy option and named a doll. One had a teapot because that was always a good line. One kept an ashtray shaped like a banana – this led to some chuckles – but it was stated that it reminded the particular lady of her first taste of one after the war was over. 'You couldn't get a real banana then – the other kind – oh, your dirty minds – they've always been around.'

Mrs Fairhurst felt well satisfied with this first session. All of them had contributed and it would look well on her report to the Central Office . . . Then she saw Mr Checket staring intently out of the window. 'Mr Checket! Mr Checket!' she called out.

'Eh, what?'

'What about your object . . . your love object? You haven't given us one?'

'A saxophone,' he replied in a half-whisper.

'A saxophone . . . well, well . . . I never knew that you played a musical instrument.'

'I don't.'

'Do you like listening to the saxophone?'

'Not particularly.'

'Did . . . did . . .' Mrs Fairhurst did not continue as Henry had turned his face back towards the garden. Mrs Fairhurst shook her head. His mind was wandering again. She felt sad about this. Sometimes, nature seemed so unkind. If only he would develop a physical debility simultaneous with this mental fading then she might be able to transfer him to the geriatric ward of a hospital. He could dream there all day. She looked at him now – his eyes glazed – staring out at the garden. She shrugged.

This was what happened if people lived little limited lives. His experience probably did not go further than the mean street that he had been born in.

For his part, Henry did not think of Dipwell Street. He never thought of it. His thoughts centred and rested in Siam. Nowadays it was advertised as Thailand, a holiday place for the rich. Exotic, beautiful, erotic.

———————————

Henry had not holidayed there . . . He had spent the best years of his manhood working on a ghastly and vile project (instigated by the Japanese) called the Siam-Burma railway.

Henry recalled the suffering, the numbers of dead and dying buried alongside that iron track. He was back there now. It was the fourth of September and the year was 1945. He was in a place called Nakhon Nayok. Impossible to forget a name like that. There was nothing romantic about the place – just a clearing in the jungle with crude huts erected by the prisoners themselves to provide protection from the monsoons. It looked and was wretched.

And how had he got to that far off spot in the first place? As a teenager in the mid 1930s he had thought even the English seaside was remote from his Midlands home. The orphanage never offered holidays. The sea had been unknown to him, let alone a jungle. He had never liked the jungle from his very first day of it. But it was in the jungle that he had met Charlie Sangster.

'I'm frightened. I feel sick,' he had said to Charlie.

'So am I, mate. I don't know whether I've shit myself or not, and right at this moment I couldn't give a fuck whether I 'ave or I ain't. Now, just you fink as though we're in a pantomime and let's get fuckin' movin'.'

'A pantomime?'

'Yeah – somefink like Jack an' the Beanstalk. Front and back-half of the cow. That's what we are. Now, what d'yer want, its head or its arse? All the same in love an' war, innit?'

Henry had taken the back part of the stretcher whilst Charlie had taken the front. Coupled this way, at the behest of the wounded and maimed of war, they began a most daring speciality act. What applause they received came from haggard faces and tired eyes – there was little laughter or joy.

Thus began many sorties for men who had been torn and rent by mortar, shrapnel and blast. When the Japanese took over their medical-centre base the two men were relieved of the stretcher. The wounded were left. Henry and Charlie were now able-bodied prisoners of war and, as such, were deployed by the special services of the Emperor Hirohito. Five years previous to this, if anyone had suggested that Henry Checket from West Bromwich and Charlie Sangster from Bermondsey would have been railway building for the Emperor of Japan, he would have been thought stark, raving mad.

Veronica Fairhurst drew his attention from the outside world by a well-timed pedagogic cough. 'Ahem! Ahem!' Henry turned to look at her. 'Ah, you're still with us, Henry.' Henry smiled and gently nodded. From the calm, beatific expression on his face Veronica Fairhurst knew full well that this was not the case. Nevertheless, she added: 'I'm so glad – we need your contribution just as much as anyone else's. Now, this time next week ... this time next week ...' Veronica was forced into a pause. Peggy Thurston had begun to make her way out without excuse or bidding. How irritating to have the conclusion ... ruined.

Veronica Fairhurst's voice changed its tone. Her question sounded harsh and metallic. 'Where are you going, Peggy?'

'It's half-past eleven.'

'I know it's half-past eleven. Sit down, dear.' Peggy Thurston continued to edge her way between the rows of chairs.

'Time for tea and a biscuit,' Peggy called out as she carefully, but deliberately, picked her way along. Progress, at her age, was full of hazard.

'Peggy, Peggy, go back to your seat and wait for a minute. Wait until I have finished. Go back to your seat, dear. I'm sorry to say this, dear . . . but if you don't go back to your seat . . . you won't get any tea. Or biscuits, so go back.'

Peggy continued her progress and muttered. 'She's never been sorry in her whole bleeding life. Never been sorry – never been sorry – never been sorry . . .' She shook her head from side to side as she talked, but continued her crab-like progress.

Veronica Fairhurst pressed on the bell attached to the wall. She pressed it firmly. She pressed it three times. The sharp ringing rasped through the room. For most of the inmates it represented alarm, fear, even excitement. A return to the arena . . . The victim continued to move.

The door opened and an ancillary wearing a green overall entered the room. She could have been a mother who was doing part-time work now that her children had grown up and left home. 'Just a little pocket-money – I help out at the home . . . with the elderly, you know.' Yes, she could have been anybody's mother apart from – apart from – the overall.

'Ah, it's you, Gladys.' Veronica greeted her then nodded to Peggy: 'It's Mrs Thurston. I'd like her to sit down. Put her back in her seat, would you?'

'Want to go to the toilet,' Peggy called out. Her voice carried as much veiled threat as Veronica's had previously done. Mrs Fairhurst made a slight hand movement and her militia ancillary froze. Peggy sniffed victory. 'Want to go to the toilet. I want to go real bad. Front and back. I don't want to share that with anybody. Not even myself. Got to keep my self-respect. People wouldn't like a mess all over the place. No, they would not . . . no, they would not . . .' She had almost reached the open door. 'I'm no chocolate drawers.'

'Let her go,' Veronica murmured to the ancillary. She closed the meeting without Peggy's or Henry's presence. Peggy was outside the room and Henry was in it.

CHAPTER

2

'Toilet, toilet, toilet,' Peggy gasped as she made her way along the corridor. Residents and staff quickly drew to one side to let her pass by. If any had looked back, he or she would have noticed Peggy edge past the illuminated lavatory sign and then, appearing to find fresh energy and agility, quickly reach a door further on. Here, she paused and glanced about her. She opened this door (which was marked 'Private'), clicked it carefully behind her, then smiled before she descended the steps that led into the bowels of the home.

The boiler room had no view of the outside world but it was warm – and secret. 'When you were over seventy, why did everybody want to know everything, yes, everything? Did you sleep well? How are you today? Did you use your waterworks before you went to bed? How was the rice pudding?' Peggy spoke out to no one but herself and her surroundings. She could afford the luxury of being vulgar, and like some comedian banned from the BBC, continued to make herself laugh. With a grunt of satisfaction she took note of her surroundings.

This was the empire of Winston Worrell – caretaker and boilerman of Restmore. It was his time for absenting himself from the building. He would be away for one hour and fifteen minutes precisely. Until Veronica Fairhurst's appointment he had always stayed on the premises throughout the day, often mingling with the elderly residents and always taking his lunch with them. His open, brown face, ready smile and white, crinkly hair gave him the appearance of a West Indian Father Christmas. Veronica Fairhurst envied his social appeal. She smiled a great deal herself but never got the sort of response that Winston received. She had called him to her office.

'You know, in a centre,' she gave the impression of chiding herself by placing a forefinger on her top lip, 'no, a home – a home of this nature – space is most important. Each and every-one of us needs individual space. Just like the pieces in a jigsaw puzzle, Mr Worrell.'

'I don't do jigsaws.' Winston Worrell knew that Veronica Fairhurst disliked him. He knew that she was about to say something foul, politely.

'Now, Mr Worrell, if you place a piece of a jigsaw puzzle in the wrong place – what does it do?'

'What *does* it do?' Winston asked, knowing that she wished to answer the question herself.

'It ruins the picture, Mr Worrell – it upsets the balance.' She paused. 'I wonder if you are following my train of thought. Are you?'

'You want me to stay down in the boiler room, keep to my own territory.'

'I wouldn't have put it quite so forcefully as that – though I'm sure that there is much to do down there – without busying yourself with the foibles of our guests here. I'm so pleased that you see my point.'

Winston Worrell saw Veronica Fairhurst's point all right but he was not pleased. He felt not unlike a refugee who for some reason had been plonked in some great tract of land that was little more than a desert. Scratch the soil, nurture the rocks, make your garden grow – but not anywhere near me. He simply smiled, nodded his head and said, 'I under-stand.'

The elderly guests at Restmore missed his presence. He supervised the cleaning of the home before most of them were awake and when they were awake he worked far beneath them in the bowels of the building. During lunch times he knew that his cavern was being used in some way. But then, he was a compassionate man and did not question who his visitors were. At all times they left the place tidy.

Peggy glanced about the basement. She noticed the new pictures, two football teams – full colour. One English, the other Italian. A small, gate-leg table nestled just below the feet of the players.

With the methodical concentration of a semi-skilled factory worker, Peggy took the kettle, filled it with water from the sink and placed it on the gas ring. She lit the gas ring, rescued the enamel teapot from behind the bucket and mop and warmed it near the gas flame. She reached down with her right hand and began to ferret about her left breast. 'Ah, there.' From somewhere about her shrunken breast she produced three tea bags. How bloody silly that you had to hide tea bags under your tits. She popped the tea bags into the teapot and sat down on one of the two chairs near the table. She waited, not impatiently. Henry was always reliable. The water would just about be boiled by the time that he arrived to join her.

She looked at the photographs on the wall and gave each player closer scrutiny. The English team had their arms folded over their chests – almost as though their hands constituted some kind of encumbrance. The Italian team sat with less physical stricture. Indeed, the picture might not have been posed at all. The English players sat with legs apart. The Italians sat with knees together – also, two of the players had an arm comfortably about the shoulder of a team mate . . . and some of them were smiling.

'A short life – a short life, a footballer's life – seventeen to twenty-eight and that's the lot. For most of them anyway,' Peggy mused. 'Why should I be feeling sorry for them? I was in the registry office two days before my seventeenth birthday. I felt lucky to be getting married. Lucky! Lucky . . . !'

She had promised to honour and obey Albert Thurston – after a month of marriage she had obeyed him but honour had not come into it.

'You're lucky to have a roof over your head, young woman, and some food in your stomach. It's no good coming crying to me. Put a bit of face-powder around your eye. You don't want all and sundry knowing about your business.' Peggy's mother had offered little comfort. She was a *girl* before she was married – now, according to her mother, she was a *young woman*. 'All men are the same,' her mother had added, ushering Peggy out of her house. Did all men punch their wives, as Albert Thruston did? Did they call them terrible names and say terrible things to them in bed, as he did? 'I'm fucking you – you cowbag, so take the lot, you hot bitch – ask me for it – you cow – go on, ask me for it ...' Then the bites – and after, the thumps in the small of the back and – 'Move over, don't touch me – I need some bloody sleep – pass me the piss-pot ...' Her humiliation continued. 'I'm working to keep you.' Albert treated his wife with less concern than he gave to the farm animals where he worked.

The onset of war, two years later, brought imprisonment and incarceration for many. Yet for Peggy Thurston it heralded a freedom she could never have hoped for, or even imagined. Albert was away – doing his bit in North Africa. Peggy had not one but two choices. She could either work at a munitions factory (the women collected and delivered by bus from the village to a larger town) or work on the land. Peggy chose the land, not for any bucolic reason, but from – from – resentment. 'Anything Albert Thurston can do – I can do just as well.'

Peggy worked alongside a group of four women. When the work was finished on one farm – they were shunted to another. At first, Peggy and the two other women had been suspicious of Miss Lamb. The class divide helped none of them. Miss Lamb was the eldest unmarried daughter of a vicar with a good living from the patronage of a wealthy peer and she spoke with an accent that fractured her vowels. Her hair was cropped like that of a man – she seemed to have no time for feminine adornment – and her top lip was darkened with a moustache an adolescent male might have envied.

After some months the girls were used to Miss Lamb's voice.

After all, she was not responsible for it. And, although she was in charge she never let the rest of them do jobs she wouldn't do herself. In short, they did everything – muck-spreading, lambing, potato-picking . . . What's more, she stood up for them.

'Don't speak to my girls like that.'

'Like what?'

'"Do this." "Do that." They're not in prison. Don't order them about! Ask!'

'Who the fucking hell do you think . . .'

'You, you need us . . . Respect us . . . or we'll go elsewhere.'

Two of the women looked forward to the return of their husbands, remembering what was good about them, and requested Vera Lynn to sing for them on the radio. Miss Lamb never mentioned a man, not even her father, and Peggy dreaded the thought of seeing Albert ever again. Given the amount of time the women were together, their long hours and exhausting work, it was surprising that they ever thought much about men.

They saw few men that were young, perhaps it was this absence that made the Italians look so attractive. Or could it have been the official warnings that women must not fraternise with prisoners of war. Things that we are not supposed to touch often develop an appeal all of their own.

Potato-picking had commenced; the field that Peggy and her three friends were working on was small – it had never been used for growing potatoes before. Three sides of the field were bordered by high hedgerows of hawthorn, crab-apple and dog-rose. The remaining side bordered the dark pine forests which borrowed space from this mining, rural area of the Midlands. Up until the onset of war the field had harboured a bull. This particular stud had long since been eaten, not even his testicles wasted.

The women wore sacks tied like aprons round their waists. With the left hand they held the sack forward – with the right hand they picked the potatoes from the ground and placed them in the sackcloth pouch. From time to time they would stretch their aching backs – and then return to stooping and picking.

Drizzling rain and a cold wind added to their discomfiture. Sometimes they would shout vulgar encouragements to one another.

'You wouldn't want a bit of lovin' after a day of this, Elsie, not even if he'd treated you to three milk stouts.'

'Ah, I'd be so bloody tired – I wouldn't know it was happening. I'd only have strength to lay my head down after this lot. Never mind trying to get my legs up.'

They paid scant attention to the prisoners of war who appeared sporadically felling the pine trees. In this war, potatoes and pit props were just as important as shells or bullets. Peggy was working on the furrow closest to the forest. She paused to stretch. She heard a strange clucking noise coming from the pine shadows. She had learned that the countryside was full of weird sounds and then . . .

'Psst – psst – p-s-s-t.'

She stared into the shadows and saw one of the Italians. He was tapping his chest like Tarzan when he first met Jane. Then he said: 'Me Valerio. Me Valerio.'

Peggy did not move. She neither feared nor respected his boldness. He walked towards her from out of the pines, reached the edge of the furrow and stopped. 'Me Valerio.'

'So what,' Peggy retorted, and stood her ground.

He smiled, shook his head and said, 'No understand.'

Peggy shrugged her shoulders and was about to commence her rhythmic bending and stretching when she noticed his out-stretched arm. There was something in the palm of his hand. He was offering her some kind of gift.

'Take, take,' he gently commanded.

There was nothing special about a pinecone. The dark pine forests were littered with them. She took it from him. 'Oh, it's . . .' She found it difficult to express her wonderment. The cone had been worked and shaped into a miniature hedge-hog – a penknife had transformed it. Peggy held it gingerly. She was not used to receiving gifts. Even as a child, her only Christmas presents were clothes. 'Thanks. Thanks.' A whistle blew, he waved and turned back into the darkness of the forest.

Three days after this clandestine meeting, Miss Lamb was drawn by nature towards the cover of a large clump of bramble. Urination was so swift and private for men, they were in no danger of exposing their buttocks to the air, and they could even converse over their shoulders whilst doing it. However, this was no time to be ruminating over fair play. Her need was urgent. She pushed her way through a small gap in the bramble. The spot she discovered would have been perfect for her. But, she saw Peggy – her legs apart, knees bent – lying there. A naked man heaved and grunted over her – Peggy whimpering – stroking the back of his hair – stroking his neck.

Miss Lamb withdrew as quickly as she could but the snapping of twigs sounded like lightning crackles. As she left she saw that the man's shirt and trousers had the oddly chequered pattern worn by prisoners of war – and she thought of Columbine in her state of shock and surprise.

'We will be here for another two or three days,' Miss Lamb distributed the apples to her workmates. It was seven a.m. and the morning was chill but alive with the call of birds. 'We are being moved on afterwards and . . .' She placed an apple in Peggy's hand as well as an envelope. She looked steadily at Peggy. 'Post for you . . . Open it later, my dear.'

There was a slight delay to the morning's work. Miss Lamb was having trouble starting the tractor. 'I'll be with you in half a shake of a donkey's dick, girls – please ignore my language.' At times such as these Miss Lamb could swear like any man. Perhaps the phrases were a little more original – but they were far from polite.

Peggy could see no address on the envelope . . . couldn't be from Albert, then . . . no typing . . . nothing official . . . She tore the envelope open. A very short note and some small packets, that was all. Peggy read: 'Dear Peggy – Please find enclosed four packets of ducks' wellingtons. If you decide to paddle again then ask your friend to wear one. Best wishes, I. A. Lamb.' Peggy took a bite from her apple and placed the note and the contraceptives in her apron pocket.

'The old pisspot's working again, girls,' Miss Lamb called out from the tractor seat as the machine shuddered, groaned and spluttered beneath her. 'I'll start from the far side – take advantage of the slope until the engine warms up.' And then, 'All right, Peggy, dear?'

'Fine, fine, Miss Lamb. We'll be right behind you. Fine! Fine! Miss Lamb . . .' Peggy shouted back.

By midday it was time to eat, time to rest. The women were too tired to talk. They bit into their sandwiches and chewed. Two of the women chewed noisily as well-fitting dentures were a luxury they could not afford.

'I must have a widdle.' Peggy rose hurriedly. 'What about that apple, Elsie. I'll take it if you don't want it.'

'Have it, love, not a case of not wanting it – I can't bite it.'

'Thanks.'

'Here, Peggy, here's mine too. My stomach's been talking to me all day and it says it doesn't want any fruit.' Miss Lamb chortled but no one else seemed to find her insides of much interest. Peggy, one apple in her pocket and one clutched in either hand, sped across the field towards some bramble bushes.

'Dear God, she's in a hurry,' murmured Elsie, 'it looks as though she might have a touch of the squits.'

'Yes, it's dreadful when one is taken like that in the countryside.' Miss Lamb sought to verify Elsie's diagnosis.

'Funny, though. Funny, though, isn't it?'

'What, Elsie, dear? What is funny?' Miss Lamb asked.

'Taking apples to the toilet with you,' Elsie observed.

'Oh, I don't know. I always have a cup of tea in there of a morning . . .' Miss Lamb was relieved when she saw Peggy's figure disappear from view.

———————

Henry Checket was not startled to hear someone talking as he
descended the basement stairs. By now, he was used to Peggy
babbling on when no one was around. Some residents shunned
her and rudely declared that she went 'loopy' from time to time.
Henry thought this unfair – a conversation with yourself would
be infinitely preferable to some that he had suffered when he
had first entered the place. As he made his way slowly down
the stairway he clung to the iron rail – moving with the sideways
approach of a crab reconnoitring the intricacies of a rock pool.

———————————

He was waiting for her . . . She gave him the apples. He removed
the rough apron from about her waist and spoke foreign endear-
ments as he kissed her throat and breasts. Peggy replied in
English – she knew that whatever he was saying it was not bad.
There was no abuse like there had been with Albert. And it was
Peggy who began unbuttoning him first . . .

Henry had reached the bottom of the steps. He saw that tears
were welling in Peggy's eyes and trickling down her cheeks. She
stared at him as though she were blind. He sat near her and said
nothing.

'Oh, Miss Lamb. Oh, Miss Lamb. They've gone – they've
moved them on.'

'I'm sorry, dear,' Henry muttered. He'd been cast in many
parts in his time.

'I don't know whether you think it was bad of me – no, I know
you don't think it was bad.'

'I'm in no position to judge you – or anyone else – no, or even
myself, for that matter.'

'Oh, it was so different; so different I might never have known.
Thank God, I do know. Something happened to *me* as well as
him. With Albert – there was nothing, nothing, except hurt . . .
just hurt. But with Valerio – that's his name, Valerio – it wasn't

rough ... but gentle ... and ... and ... I don't know ... afterwards he cradled me and stroked me as though I were a child ... and he was ... he was as tender as a woman.'

'Then he was a real man, Peggy.'

'I'm glad I've known one, then. I don't think that I married one. He's not even a friend let alone the other thing.'

'You can do without the other thing – but I sometimes wonder whether you can do without a friend.'

'You're a good friend to me, Miss Lamb. The first true friend I've had. You're more than a mother to me.'

'I'm not old enough to be your mum. The kettle is boiling. I'll make us both a cup of tea. You take two spoons of sugar, don't you?' Henry Checket sugared Peggy's tea without waiting for a reply.

'I wish you wouldn't stare at me like that, Henry. It makes me feel as though frog spawn is coming out of my ears.' Peggy sipped her tea noisily. 'I've got some biscuits somewhere ... digestives ... now where are the bloody things? Can't see for looking. Got tears in me eyes.'

'It must be smoke. It must be smoke from the boiler that's been making your eyes water,' Henry said quietly.

CHAPTER

3

Veronica Fairhurst carried on working as though she were unaware of the guest in her office. She made three long telephone calls during which she did a lot of talking and very little listening. She signed several letters. She scrutinised all working hours that the ancillary helps had claimed for – she filled in forms. It was as though Henry Checket were in the room for decoration: a representation of the ageing human form. He had sat there, at her bidding, for almost half an hour. For some reason it irked her to see him staring out of the window at the moment that she was ready to attend to him. 'Mr Checket! Mr Checket! Mr Checket, are you with us?'

'Yes, I am.' Henry turned his gaze from outside to inside.

'Yes, I'm with you.' His voice was faint, as if he might fade away at any minute. Mrs Fairhurst picked up a biro and held it over a sheet of paper before her on the desk. Henry thought that she held the biro as if it were a dart. It looked lethal.

'What day is it, Mr Checket?'

'Day? Day? It's reasonably warm, a little cloud but not unpleasant. Right for the time of year, I suppose.' Henry looked out of the window for confirmation.

'No, no . . . I mean the day of the week. Is it Monday, Tuesday, Wednesday?' Mrs Fairhurst's tone hardened. 'The day of the week is what I want, Mr Checket.'

'Does it matter?' Henry answered vaguely and continued to look out of the window.

'You don't know?' This assumption seemed to please Mrs Fairhurst. 'And what month is it?' Henry remained silent. 'And what year is it, Mr Checket? What year?' Mrs Fairhurst's voice grew in strength.

Henry turned to look at her and noticed an angry red flush that decorated her neck. He sought to calm her.

'Day? Month? Week? Year? We can't defeat time, can we? It carries all of us with it and sometimes we hardly seem to notice it.'

'What is the name of the Queen's sister? Who is our prime minister?' Mrs Fairhurst wrote something on the paper as Henry failed to answer any of her questions. 'What year were you born? How old are you? I don't believe you're trying, Mr Checket.'

'In the Tower Ballroom at Blackpool there is a great big mirrored globe that hangs from the high ceiling. When the lights go down and couples take to the dance floor it spins this way and that. It lights up bits of faces and everybody seems to be flickering as though the film had got stuck at the pictures . . .'

'Yes, I'm sure, Mr Checket – yes, I'm sure.' Mrs Fairhurst cut in on Henry's reverie. He was disappointed that she did not seem curious. 'Ah, Gladys.' Mrs Fairhurst greeted the green-overalled lady who tapped and opened the door simultaneously.

'Could you come for a moment, Mrs Fairhurst. I'm so sorry to burst in like this. It's Mrs Thurston. We're having trouble with her.'

Mrs Fairhurst flung the biro at the desk top. Henry watched as it bounced off the surface and onto the floor. Mrs Fairhurst ignored it and followed her ancillary, 'Oh, that woman' – somehow she managed to make this phrase sound abusive.

Henry rose slowly from his seat near the window. He picked up the biro from the carpet and sat with some deliberation on Mrs Fairhurst's chair. 'It's Tuesday – all day. It's October, 1987. December the tenth, 1918 I was born.' He quietly reeled off all the answers to her previous questions. Henry thought that Mrs Fairhurst was a fool and he did not consider that he had sufficient time left to answer the questions of fools.

Henry had no qualms about studying the piece of paper on Mrs Fairhurst's desk. He assumed she had been writing about him and, if that was the case, wasn't he entitled to look at what she had written? The sheet of paper did not provide Henry with any enlightenment about himself but did give a very odd insight into Mrs Fairhurst. The page was full of strange, meaningless doodles. He was about to move back to his former seat when a typed letter caught his attention.

Re: Henry Checket
Peggy Thurston

Dear Mrs Fairhurst,
Thank you for your letter and the detailed information with regard to the above clients. I am afraid that I cannot put forward a case for psychiatric review so swiftly after the last one. Perhaps I could consider it for some time in the New Year. Certainly, it would be impossible before Christmas.

I am sure that you must realise that a transfer to a psycho-geriatric ward would be problematic without this kind of clinical assessment. Of course, your observations about Mr Checket and Mrs Thurston will be carefully noted and given the deepest consideration. And, perhaps, they are both misplaced at Restmore Haven. However, I would remind you that you (or I, for that matter) are not psychiatrists. However, I do value and take into account your viewpoint.

I think, in the circumstances, it would be better if we discussed both clients when I visit on November 27th. If we can sort out some particular points at this informal meeting I would suggest a case conference at a date not too long after this.

Let me take this opportunity of congratulating you on the success of your Autumn Fayre. The mayor was particularly impressed – in his letter to me he stressed

that the care of the elderly and animal welfare were
his two pet charities.

I look forward to seeing you on the 27th.

Yours sincerely,

Alisdair J. McClennon (P.O.M.H.)

'God, she's trying to get rid of us. Put Peggy and me in the looney
bin. Must let Peggy know about this. She's up with Peggy now.
Hope Peggy doesn't play her up too much,' Henry muttered as
he got up from behind the desk – as an afterthought, entirely out
of character – he seized the biro from the desk and hurled it at
the wall with some force, as though wreaking vengeance on an
imaginary dartboard.

'Now, Peggy, Peggy, there's no need to be silly over just one
faded photograph. And why have you sellotaped it on to the wall?
And where did you get it from? Does it belong to you?' Veronica
Fairhurst spoke in saccharine tones as the two ancillaries edged
slowly towards the photograph.

Peggy sat silent on her bed. 'I know your game. She croons on
while one of you two snatch my picture. Leave it. Stay where you
are. It's mine.'

Mrs Fairhurst stopped her cohorts with a slight movement of
her hand. 'Gladys says she thinks you have taken it from Miss
Whittaker's room. You might have thought it was yours at the
time of taking it. So no one will be cross with you if you let
us have it back. After all, you wouldn't want to take something
from a lady who's passed on. Miss Whittaker's nearest and
dearest are coming to collect all her things tomorrow. You
wouldn't want to steal from the . . . from the . . .' Mrs Fairhurst
measured her tone carefully. '. . . from the dead, Peggy, would
you?'

'It's mine. Sod off,' Peggy snapped and clutched her arms about her knees as she brought them up to her chin.

'Oh, Mrs Fairhurst, how can that be true', Gladys intervened, 'we know that Miss Whittaker and all her family had the closest affiliations with the cloth. Her father was a verger and her brother a vicar – Mrs Thurston couldn't have known . . .'

'Please don't interrupt, Gladys,' said Veronica Fairhurst before her amateur detective could complete her charge. 'Please. Thank you.' She took up the interrogation of Peggy herself. She scrutinised the photograph. A vicar – small in stature, stood at the entrance of his manse. By his side stood a tall, angular woman, whose broad shoulders and large arms looked awkward in a summer dress.

'Now, Peggy, my dear. Who is this in the picture?'

'It's Larry.'

'Larry, is it? Larry!' Veronica Fairhurst paused to give time for her ancillaries to snigger – after all their work had to have some compensations. 'Is that the name of the gentleman – Larry? Was the vicar's name Larry?'

'Don't know any vicars. I got married at the registry, and I'm not dead yet – so, I'm not about to meet one.'

Mrs Fairhurst raised both her arms in mock horror and with a movement of her head indicated that she and her workers should leave the room. 'Hopeless, hopeless,' she murmured. 'Hopeless. Don't worry, girls – one can only do so much for Peggy . . . hopeless . . . hopeless.' She continued murmuring and tut-tutting as she walked away down the corridor.

Henry stood quite still in the curtained recess and watched Mrs Fairhurst negotiate the corner with her entourage, before stepping from behind the fire buckets. He was used to making himself invisible. The corridor was clear. He tapped on Peggy's door.

'Come in,' bawled Peggy. It would not be Veronica Fairhurst or her cohorts whose entrance was always the same. There would be a short knock – and before she could answer – the door would open and a voice would say, 'It's only me,' as if to check the gas

meter. Peggy was glad to see Henry hovering in the doorway.
'Come in, come in. I don't bite. Close the door behind you.'

'Fairhurst's been here. She wanted to take my photograph
from me. Wanted to take it away.'

'Who is it?' Henry looked at the sepia-tinted picture. 'It's
Larry – you know, my friend Miss Lamb.'

'Ah ... ah ... yes.' Henry looked at that lady and compre-
hended fully.

'She was golden to me. That's her dad she's with. She didn't
like him all that much. She was a disappointment to him. She told
me so herself.'

'Funny name for a girl – Larry,' Henry ruminated aloud.

'Oh, I gave it to her. You see, I'd often eat with her of an evening after working all day. We'd play cards and listen to the radio.
She liked crib. Taught me to play it. She even had a dartboard.
There weren't many ladies who played darts then – or crib, for
that matter. But if we were playing darts or crib no matter how
close the game was between us, we'd have to stop for "Toytown".'

'Toytown?'

'Yes. It was on the wireless. It was a children's programme.
Miss Lamb was ever so sensible but she could be like a child at
times. Larry the Lamb was the main character – so I called her
"Larry". I think she liked it better than her own name.'

'What was her name?'

'Imogen.'

'Lord, I'm not surprised that she preferred "Larry".' Henry
shuffled awkwardly on his chair and added, 'She's trying to get
rid of us, you and me.'

'Eh, eh, what you say? She's dead, Henry. Larry's dead.'

'No, I mean Veronica Fairhurst. She's trying to get rid of us.'

'What do you think she can bloody do? Wave a magic wand and
wait for us to disappear?' Peggy could not disguise the horror and
contempt from her tone. Henry did tend to bleat at times.

'It's serious. She wants to put us in the looney bin for the old.'

'I'm old, but I'm not looney. She'll have to carry me on a
stretcher if she wants to get me there.' This time Peggy spoke

with less confidence. 'There's some biscuits in the top drawer. Nearer you, the one near the dresser. Chocolate digestive – pass me one as well.' Peggy drew herself up to a more upright, sitting position on the bed. 'How do you know?'

'Saw a letter on her desk, didn't I? Read it for myself.'

'Well, I suppose we'll have to behave ourselves now, Henry.'

'I do behave.'

'No, I mean, behave for her. Yes, Mrs Fairhurst. No, Mrs Fairhurst. Three bags full, Mrs Fairhurst. Dance to your tune, Mrs Fairhurst. Tra-la-la.'

'We'll fight her,' Henry replied, quietly and defiantly.

'And when the fight is over . . . That's what they used to say on the wireless.' Peggy nibbled her biscuit. 'Once, when we were playing crib, Dorothy Squires was singing.'

'Yes, she had a good strong voice.'

'"Coming Home My Darling" – that's what she was singing. And I started to cry. Sobbing and blubbering, I went into a right caterwaul, I can tell you. Miss Lamb was upset for me. She patted the back of my hand. "Never mind, Peggy, my dear, never mind. He'll soon be with you again." Course I howled louder when she said that because I didn't want to see him again. I'd missed Albert Thurston as much as I'd miss arthritis. In fact, I'd rather have lived with arthritis than him. I told Miss Lamb, I told her straight. She didn't blink; just stared ahead of her and moved her head from side to side. "What sort of peace have we got to look forward to . . . you and me . . . What sort of peace? And if we have any say, which we do not . . . if we had any say, Peggy . . . how would we fashion it?"'

'She sounds sweet,' said Henry non-committally.

'Well, she wasn't a lump of sugar. I wouldn't say that she was sweet. But she was good. She clicked the wireless off when the song ended and we both sat there and cried together.'

'I wonder who was crying for who?' Henry pondered aloud.

'Finish your biscuit,' Peggy replied.

CHAPTER
4

Henry had not forgotten to go down for his evening meal. He had decided that he did not want it. Perhaps Peggy's chocolate biscuits had taken away his appetite. It was also Thursday, and this was a time when he listened to 'Big Band Favourites' on the radio. It was presented in a cloying, nostalgic way which Henry disliked. First, there was something by Stan Kenton and His Orchestra, and then half way through Glenn Miller and his 'String of Pearls' he had switched the radio off. He lay on his bed, clasped his hands behind his neck and stared fixedly at the ceiling. One of the best things about old age was that you could dream when you wanted to. You didn't have to go to sleep or even close your eyes.

'I can't think, for the life of me, what Charlie saw in saxophones. I don't like the sound of them. No, I don't, not separately or together. He'd done enough shit jobs, said he was going to be an artist. All his family worked in the docks, perhaps that's where he got his swearing from . . . "but work was work, Charlie." That's what I used to say to him . . . oh, Charlie, oh, dear.' The sigh transported him, with its mixture of ecstasy and regret.

Within the limits of both Henry's and Charlie's experience no employers had been that good. You couldn't say that they were good at all. But none, not even the meanest ratbag, could have been worse than the Emperor of Japan.

The rules of labour were quite simple. You worked. You ate little. If you were unfit then you died. Death amongst co-workers was commonplace, so commonplace that some prisoners accepted it too easily, almost as some kind of relief from life. Not Charlie Sangster. Charlie was a survivor. At least, that is what he always said he was when he talked to Henry.

'Go on, eat 'em. Brush the dirt off 'em. Chew 'em and think of eel and mash.'

'What are they?' Henry had asked lamely as he brushed the earth off the strange, stringy looking, unappetising roots.

'Christ only knows, I don't. But the Siamese eat 'em, I've seen 'em and we've got to keep goin'.'

'What for?' Henry had chewed on the root. He had swallowed and winced at its bitter taste. 'What's in it for us? What's in it for you?'

'When I'm out of all this, d'you know what I'm going to do?' Charlie did not wait for a reply but passed Henry another root. 'Here, 'ave anover one. I'll tell yer what I'm goin' to do. I'm goin' to play the saxophone. I'll play it in a big band. Then after some spots and a bit of luck . . . I might even take pot luck in America. Can you see me with Jimmy Dorsey?' He had placed his arm around Henry's shoulder and had drawn him to him. 'Wouldn't fit in wiv Ivy Benson's lot, us two, would we?'

'Do you think we'll ever get out of here, Charlie?'

'Dunno, I dunno. But yer gotta 'ave somefink to look forward to, ain't yer?' Charlie had let his hand rove about Henry's nipple. 'Don't like bein' on me own.'

And later, on their bed of stinking palm leaves and grasses, Henry had said, 'You know, Charlie, we could get sent to prison back home for what we did last night.'

'We're already in fuckin' prison, so I don't give a piss. I just thank God I've got a bit of strength still left in me tassle. And I'm glad that yer like it. Yer do, don't yer?'

'Yes.'

'Come 'ere, then. Let's get close. Yer not like an old bag to me, Henry. I'd do it wiv you wherever I was. Just move round a bit . . . oh . . . oh. Apart from all this . . . oh . . . I do like yer. Oh . . . oh . . . that's it, good . . . go . . . on, slowly, boy, go . . . on . . . fuckin' lovely.'

Some prisoners lived and some died. Henry and Charlie (in the face of extreme adversity) somehow managed to live and sometimes laugh. And, in spite of, not because of their environment, they also managed to love.

Henry stared at the stone petals decorating the centre of his bedroom ceiling and thought more carefully on this matter of love. Sex, for him without love, was meaningless. Yet . . . and yet . . . he could cope with love without sex. Strangely, he found this thought funny. He chuckled aloud over it. His own laughter broke his reverie. This was as well, as he could hear whispering tones outside his door. He knew the tones. He was familiar with the cadences and inflections of this voice.

'Lamb! Lamb! Lamb! Are you in there. Are you in? It's me. Peggy. Are you in?'

Henry heaved his cumbersome, diamond-shaped frame from off the bed and opened the door just wide enough for his visitor to sidle into the room. He closed the door. She sat on his bed and he lowered himself into the loom armchair.

'That thing needs oiling,' said Peggy, pointing to the chair. 'Well, are you going to let her get away with it?'

'Eh, what d'you say, Peggy?' Henry asked.

'Fairhurst! Fairhurst! Are we going to let her chuck us out. Throw us in the looney bin. Swim around in one of those goldfish bowls with a crowd of old dimwits.'

'I think that you are being a little harsh, Peggy, my dear.'

'Harsh! Harsh! Me, harsh? What's Fairhurst, then, if she's not harsh?'

'Oh, I was thinking of the old people in the hospitals, not her,' said Henry.

'Well, I didn't mean any offence to them. But we're not ready to join 'em.' Peggy paused here and stared at Henry in a challenging fashion. 'At least, I'm not ready to join them. Are you?'

'No, I'm not,' Henry declared flatly.

'What are we going to do? How can we beat her?'

'I suppose we'll have to conform, conform better than anybody else.' Henry sighed at his own insight.

'Conform?'

'Oh, behave. We have to behave as she wants us to. We have to be well-behaved.'

'You make it sound as though we are in a bloody seal-house. I'm not balancing a ball on my nose for that cow.'

'Well, we have to play her game for a while – and play it well or she'll have us out of here.'

'Not part us – not separate us . . . ?' Much to Henry's astonishment Peggy began to cry. 'Oh, Lamb, you're all I've got. You're all I've got. You're no raving beauty, Christ knows, you're not . . . but I'm used to you . . . and . . .' Peggy began crying again.

Henry began to wonder if Peggy was becoming a little dotty. She called him Lamb now, and there could hardly be any physical resemblance between him and that good lady. For his part, he did not mind the confusion if that is what it was.

'She won't part us.' Henry spoke flatly, in a matter of fact way. Peggy stopped crying immediately, then got off the bed and pulled up the left leg of her stocking which always seemed to want to settle about her ankle. Henry averted his eyes. He was aware that in some odd way he had committed himself to Peggy. He felt quite elated about this.

'I'd better be off, now,' said Peggy. 'Shall I give you a kiss before I go?'

'Oh!' Henry was disconcerted by this new development. But Peggy quickly reassured him. 'Only on the cheek. Only on the cheek. Like we used to. Bend your head down. I can't reach you. I'm not going to stand on the bed.' Henry bent his head and shoulders in dutiful fashion.

'There,' said Peggy, after she had placed a dry mouth to the side of his face. This was the first physical endearment he had received in over thirty years. And Henry felt it was not entirely without meaning.

Peggy left quietly and enjoyed making her way back to her own room unnoticed. Old age was not devoid of thrills and the forthcoming struggle offered adventure and a sense of liberation.

When the American soldiers had entered the hut, they found twelve bodies amongst the palms, grasses and excrement. There was the insistent buzzing of many flies who found this hell-hole a haven. The stench was so overpowering that two of the liberators retched and vomited. Just three of the twelve bodies were alive – or at least they were breathing. Henry was delirious – he was suffering from typhoid, amoebic dysentery and beri-beri. He could answer questions but not coherently. His answers made no sense to his questioners. The young Canadian died as he was being shuttled into the ambulance van. Charlie lay next to Henry comatose – strange rattling sounds coming from his throat. Henry watched as two flies crawled over Charlie's face. They moved about his features like explorers who knew there were no dangers on the territory. There were no defences.

It couldn't be Charlie – Henry thought – no, it couldn't be. Charlie wouldn't allow anyone to walk all over him like that. No, Charlie was still around somewhere.

Four months later the hospital authorities informed Henry that Charlie was dead.

Henry could not accept this. On demobilisation he began his search for his friend. He moved from town to town, from dance hall to dance hall and studied the saxophone players in England. Eventually Henry found he began to hate the sound of the instrument. As its popularity waned Henry's search became less intense. He had never chosen to settle in London. He just found himself there – just as he had ended up in Thailand. It was no good planning too far ahead.

CHAPTER

5

By pressing the second button on the machine next to his telephone, Alisdair McClennon practised a deceit. His index finger illuminated a sign outside his door which read: Engaged. This was not true. He sat alone and unworking, and drank his mid-morning cup of coffee. Eleven o'clock was a good time for a cup of coffee and a cigarette. As Principal Officer of Mental Health he knew that neither the black coffee nor the untipped cigarette was good for him. He inhaled and then sipped and shrugged away the thought. He looked at the button that protected his privacy with satisfaction. Gadgets such as this would save or destroy us all some day.

In this gloomy, philosophical train of thought he re-read his colleague's letter, yet another invitation to attend a wedding. Sons or daughters were always getting married – now that he was approaching sixty these wedding invitations had increased. Alisdair disliked weddings – for the first time he penned a refusal which he tempered by adding the rail fare to the cheque he enclosed as a present. He still felt a little guilty. He was very fond of this colleague but not interested in his relatives. He sighed and pressed the other button. It buzzed.

As though her eyes had been riveted to the sign outside in the corridor and as though Alisdair's buzzer was the crack of a starting pistol, Veronica Fairhurst opened the door. She spoke before Alisdair had any time for formal greeting.

'Today – just this morning – they both informed me that they were getting married. Did you ever hear of anything so absurd – it's painful it really is.'

'What!' said Alisdair, taken aback by Veronica Fairhurst's opening salvo. Could she have seen his colleague's note? Such telepathy . . .

'Good morning, do sit down, Veronica.' Alisdair sought to formalise the meeting and collect his thoughts.

'They plan to marry in the New Year. Of course, I took neither of them seriously. I told them it was a big step. All I got back was a retort from Mrs Thurston that she had done a lot of high-jumping in her time and any step – big or little held no worries. Then cackles from her and nods and smiles from Mr Checket. Really, they are quite demented. Of course, I shan't give them permission.'

Alisdair opened the file on his desk, stubbed out his cigarette and decided to let the rest of his coffee go cold. 'If they do, Veronica, they won't need your permission. At their age they can marry quite freely.' Alisdair looked up from his papers. 'I gather you feel the need of intervention from me – that is – that is with regard to Mrs Thurston and Mr Checket.'

'Not intervention, Mr McClennon,' Alisdair noted the intensity of Veronica Fairhurst's gaze. Her eyes bulged. Did she have some kind of thyroid problem? Or was it her green eye-shadow? 'Not intervention. I need your help.'

Alisdair realised that this request meant Veronica Fairhurst wanted him to do her bidding. He had studied Henry's and Peggy's notes and still felt that he could not respect her wishes. She managed Restmore well. Often he had heard her say, 'Everyone here is part of my family'; to him, something of an indictment. He would not want to be part of 'her family', whatever the situation. He was not surprised that Henry and Peggy did not fit in or behave as Mrs Fairhurst wanted.

He stroked his beard. 'The psychiatrist's report – when was it, the twenty-fourth of November – doesn't give any indication that the degree of senility is anywhere near as advanced as you have made out. There is really very little that we could act on.'

'Ah, but he's not in the front line, is he?'

'Pardon?'

'Dr Clayton – this psychiatrist – he's not in the front line. He doesn't have to deal with these two day by day.'

'I have known Margaret Clayton for many years. She has known many "front lines" as you put it.' Alisdair disliked the imagery of warfare applied to any aspects of care. Nevertheless, Veronica Fairhurst continued.

'So it's me that has to do all the trouble-shooting. I hadn't realised Dr Clayton was a woman.' For some reason the inflection of Veronica's voice made the point that the gender seemed inappropriate to the status.

'She is a good doctor,' Alisdair replied. He then leaned back to hear of Henry and Peggy's misdeeds which largely consisted of their opting out of the routines and activities Veronica instigated. He could not see how their obduracy could cause such mayhem.

'I wonder if she has gone into their social backgrounds sufficiently? It's much more than the here and now that affect the elderly. Their past comes under focus.' Veronica delivered this as information. Alisdair thought she sounded like a fundamentalist preacher. He felt discomfort not only from her tone but from wind. He burped then coughed. 'Their past?' he enquired innocently as if he knew nothing. 'At their age, I suppose, there must be a lot of it. The past, I mean.'

'Well, I ask you, what sort of woman leaves her husband and child? And the husband not being home more than eighteen months after the war is over. What kind of woman is that? The patriotism shared by 90 per cent of the population at that time didn't seem to have permeated Peggy Thurston.' Veronica waited for some response from Alisdair. He coughed again.

'Mm ... mm ... mm – I suppose it's a question of how it is viewed. Facts often change their meaning when they are presented differently. It's a bit like belief. As for Mrs Thurston, I believe a great part of what you have said is open to question. I've looked into the details.' He held up his hand as Veronica Fairhurst attempted to interrupt him. 'Please. Let me finish. When Peggy left her husband did you know her child was already dead? The baby died when it was seventeen days old. She never left the hospital with it. After that she stayed with her husband for a further fortnight.'

'But she deserted him. She deserted her husband,' Veronica insisted vehemently.

Alisdair nodded his head. 'Yes, that's true. I think she had little choice. When she was admitted to hospital, just one day before the birth of her baby girl, Mrs Thurston was found to have severe bruising about neck and breasts. Her buttocks were striped with red and blue weals – indications of recent beatings – and two fingers of her right hand were dislocated. It was recorded as a domestic quarrel.'

'Mr McClennon, they were very different times. Marriage was sacred then . . . and . . .'

'I can see very little sanctity in such cruelty. In fact, I can see none. And what a patriotic legacy he brought back.' Alisdair could not keep the anger from his voice.

'Was there money involved?' Veronica enquired.

'No, Peggy inherited only syphilis from her husband. So did her baby girl. The child was born deaf and blind. Perhaps its early demise was a mercy. I can't know. Blood has always been a battlefield – that child was destroyed by the war even before she was conceived.'

'So all that money was left to her by that woman? By Miss Lamb?'

'Yes, but fourteen thousand pounds is not a great amount nowadays. But to the point, Veronica; I cannot surmise what sort of woman Peggy is – not from these notes. What I *can* surmise is that there must have been an enormous degree of determination and strength in her merely for her to have survived for so long. No, we cannot use her past against her.'

'Well, if you put it like that, I suppose not. But what of the present? Here she is proposing marriage to an octogenarian ex-vagrant. Never been married before, lived like a . . .' Alisdair stopped listening to Veronica's grinding tones. He had read and re-read Henry's notes – he had delved further than the notes. He felt that he knew Henry Checket and, while Veronica Fairhurst talked on, he conceived his own picture but kept his thoughts and his images to himself.

The rehabilitation officer's voice was so posh that the sounds he made seemed to fracture Henry's eardrums. Henry told himself that 'orff' was 'off' and that 'halp' was 'help'.

'Well, we will soon have you off back home now, Mr Checket. Back to old England. I dare say you'll be glad to get back after your ghastly time here. I might say that I think that you are lucky to be alive.' Henry smiled at the fresh-faced, well-intentioned officer. Although he spoke the same language, Henry's diverse social experience both before and during his internment as a prisoner of war made him feel the officer might well have arrived from another planet rather than having roots in the same country as himself.

'Now, as to your relatives, wife, children, parents – perhaps you could give me some details. Of course, you will be writing yourself – but there's no harm in us dropping a line or two. Just to prepare the way for your home-coming. I'll bet they'll be jolly pleased to see you, and I dare say you'll be more than happy to be re-united with them. Now, if you will just give me . . .'

'I don't have any, sir.'

'I beg your pardon.' The officer placed the pencil back on his desk as he spoke.

'Of what you said. Wife, relatives and all that. I was from an orphanage, you see. I'm not legitimate.'

'But surely, you will have *some* people to go back to . . . friends . . . that sort of thing.' There was now genuine concern in the young officer's tone.

'No, there's nobody I knew before that will want to see me.

Not specially anyhow. I don't specially want to see them either, so there's no love lost.'

'I'll just go through the demobilisation form, then – your effort and that of many others like yourself has not gone entirely unforgotten, you know. If there is no one that you wish to contact then we can proceed.'

'There is someone, sir. Mr Sangster – Mr Charlie Sangster – you see, me and him were taken together. I seem to have lost all trace of him here in the base hospital. I remember talking with him in the hut – that was before our lads found us. He must be here somewhere – mustn't he?' There was more than pleading to Henry's question but the officer ignored his desperation. He said: 'What is his name – Sangster – Charles Sangster?'

'Yes, that's it. That's it.'

'If you'll wait a minute – I'll just check the reception file. I won't keep you long.' Henry watched him go through into a smaller office. He caught a glimpse of a woman typing at a desk. They were rare sights to him – women – and typewriters. This was a strange new world.

The officer returned with a sheet of paper, accompanied by the lady typist who gave Henry a cup of tea – it had milk and sugar in it. The officer sat behind his desk and the lady stood next to Henry after she had handed him his tea. It was a pleasure to come across such nice people. And then, the officer spoke without looking up from his desk.

'I'm afraid he's dead. Your friend Mr Sangster is dead. I'm sorry.'

'Oh, no, there's been a mistake,' Henry laughed nervously. 'Not Charlie, he was a survivor. He can't be gone.'

'Mr Sangster is dead. He was dead at the time you were discovered.'

'Dead! Charlie dead!!' Henry exclaimed. 'Oh, oh, no, you must have mixed him up with somebody else. Not Charlie, no, not Charlie.'

'Have another sip of tea, my dear,' the woman placated him.

'All the men in the hut, the men who were with you have been accounted for. Mr Sangster died of acute jaundice and severe malnutrition. He was identified by one of the officers. I'm sorry about this, Mr Checket, truly I am.' Henry had begun to make his way out of the room. He moved slowly, as though his feet were weighted by the news he had received. The young officer scribbled something on a piece of paper and called out. 'Mr Checket – Mr Checket. Here, here is Mr Sangster's home address. It's a London address. Perhaps you might want to call . . . after a time.'

He handed Henry the paper. 'This war has been a bastard, Mr Checket. A bastard.'

To his surprise Henry answered, 'There's worse things than being a bastard, sir. I should know, shouldn't I?'

———————

'I ought to know if anyone should, shouldn't I?'

'What? What?' Alisdair spoke much too loudly as Veronica Fairhurst's insistent voice crashed through his thoughts.

'Well, I wouldn't want to be critical of colleagues in higher positions, but I do think that my observations ought to carry more weight. Everyone needs to be valued. Every single point of mine with regard to Mrs Thurston and Mr Checket has been ignored.' Veronica spoke as though she had been the recipient of some dreadful miscarriage of justice.

'I don't think that you need worry about our valuing your effort, Veronica.' (Alisdair had wanted to say, 'We are paid to care,' but chose not to take this risk.) Instead, he smiled a bright, professional smile and said, 'I have decided to see them myself.'

'Oh, – do – ' Veronica chirped. She took a diary out of her handbag. 'You can see them in my office if you wish. Let me see about times and dates. I do like to . . .'

'Oh, don't bother, Mrs Fairhurst. Please don't worry. I think I'll see them informally. I'll call on a Saturday. There are at least four or five weekends before Christmas.'

'But I'm not there every Saturday. Sometime I take a long weekend. Veronica continued to flick the pages of her diary, indicating that she had not taken Alisdair's suggestion seriously.

'We all need our time off, Mrs Fairhurst. But I'll still come on a Saturday.' He chuckled, 'After all, it's not as though I'm going to observe you. I know how well you do your job. I know what a lot you put into it.' But what about your feelings, he said to himself as he added, 'I do know how much you care about these things.'

Defeated, she closed the diary firmly and popped it into her handbag. She snapped the clasp shut with a brisk hand movement so that it emitted a 'click' that was louder than usual. 'As you wish, Alisdair. I thought I'd take my lunch in the canteen here. Are you going to eat . . .'

'I'd love to. Nothing I'd like better – but I'm afraid I'm down for a working lunch today.' Alisdair rose from his chair and went round to the side of his desk, indicating that it was time for Veronica to leave. As she rose and made her way towards the door, he swiftly overtook her and opened it. Courtesy had always been one of his strategies.

Veronica paused in the open door and said in nonchalant fashion, 'Well, I'll see you when I see you, then.'

Alisdair closed the door and lit a cigarette.

The restaurant below the Social Services (like almost everything else in the borough) had been privatised. Veronica approved. Now the cafeteria had a look of 'class' about it. It was even possible to take a glass of wine with one's meal. She took a tray and glided gracefully along the passage way. She viewed the food carefully. She would start with mackerel mousse and toast, on to lamb chops with broccoli and sauté potatoes, lemon sorbet, and then some brie with oatmeal biscuits. She chose a glass of dry French wine to help it all along. There was a pause when she reached the cashier. Veronica looked about the restaurant. She noted with gratification that no other woman was wearing a fur coat but herself. There was a man with a little fur decorating one of those vile bomber jackets but Veronica dismissed this as affectation.

She turned to the cashier who was waiting, patient but bored.

'Oh, put this on Mr McClennon's account. I'm his guest.' Veronica picked up her tray to leave. The cashier's gentle hand restrained her.

'Could I have your name, please?'

'Mrs Veronica Fairhurst.'

'I'm sorry, Mr McClennon has no one of that name on his list for today. That will be eight pounds fifty, please.' The cashier looked down at the buttons of her till as she spoke. 'I can ask someone to ring up and check, if you like.'

'No, don't. I can claim later.' Veronica did not seek further embarrassment and watched her ten-pound note disappear. She felt as though she had bought a share in the restaurant as she put the change in her purse.

She was pleased to see one of the new deputies who was sitting alone. Veronica had mixed feelings about women assuming high places in the hierarchy – but ever practical she would feed where the bee sucked.

'Do you mind if I join you?' The woman she addressed was in her late thirties, wearing dungarees, and a brown woollen pullover. There were three badges on her pullover but Veronica could not make out what each stood for.

'Please do.' The fresh-faced woman with short-cropped hair gestured to Veronica.

Veronica took off her coat and draped it about the back of her chair. Conversation did not flow easily. The woman did not seem too keen to talk about her own work or Veronica's. On the subject of families, usually a good opener, she hardly seemed to be listening. Veronica had talked of her husband, of how his work as a dentist was stressful and they both of them needed to get away most weekends to their cottage in Essex. 'Of course, he writes, too. He's published two books.' The woman murmured appreciatively between mouthfuls of lentil soup during Veronica's soliloquy. Veronica still believed a dental technician was a dentist and that two pamphlets on the care of false teeth justified her claim that he was a writer. It was all a question of priority.

Veronica concentrated on her mackerel. There was silence. Her dining partner's meal was austere in the extreme. The lentil soup was finished and now the woman was digging into a jacket potato stuffed with cheese. Veronica had made the running – better wait and see if her partner might want to respond in some way. Conversation hummed about her but at her own table there was only the chink of cutlery and the mastication of food. Veronica was beginning to think that she might as well have chosen to share her meal with a cow when suddenly the woman spoke.

'What fur is that? Your coat – what is it?'

'Oh, oh, it's not fur. Everyone's fooled by it. Don't feel put out. It's simulated ocelot.'

'I don't suppose there are any real ocelots left.' The woman picked up the skin of her potato with her fingers and ate it as though she were walking along the street. 'I had a friend who wore a coat like that once. She was on holiday in Norfolk.'

'Oh, really?' Veronica felt that the mealtime might be brightening a little.

'Yes, she was shot in the thigh. It's a wonder she didn't die. The shot pierced her artery.'

'How dreadful for her. Did they take much money from her?'

'Oh, no – no. It wasn't a mugging. It was a case of mistaken identity.'

'Good Lord!' Veronica exclaimed.

'Yes, she was crawling around near this stream looking for wild iris and some marksmen mistook her for a coypu.'

'Pardon?' Veronica felt a little faint. She sipped her wine. 'Pardon me?'

'They mistook her for a coypu. It's a huge rodent that was introduced to this country some years ago – from South America I think. They're increasing year by year, so there is a campaign on to reduce their numbers.'

'Well, I hope that she is all right, now.'

'Oh, yes, she's back at work again – bit of a limp but nothing serious.' The woman stood and gave Veronica a cheerful smile. 'Well, I must get back. Nice meeting you.'

'It's been a pleasure.' Veronica watched the woman leave the restaurant. Not only did the woman dress like a farm labourer, talk like one, but she walked like one as well. With a huge sigh Veronica began to carve her lamb chops.

Alisdair decided to avoid the lift when he left his office and made for the back stairway of the building. He did not wish to have a chance meeting with Veronica Fairhurst and there was no possibility of bumping into her in the café he usually frequented for his midday meal. He stumbled as he hurried down the staircase. Alisdair, not mindful of his age or rotund shape, wore an expensive, well-cut suit similar to those of other men who held positions like his own, yet, it was probably his choice of footwear which led to the sharp pain in his ankle. He wore calf-length boots with zips up the sides. The heels on the boots added to his stature but did little for his sense of balance. They would have suited a country and western singer much better but they appealed to the non-creative side of Alisdair's nature. As did the Sultan's Moon café.

The café's origins were only half-evident. The midday menu, which included three different kinds of kebab with rice and salad also catered for a wider and perhaps less adventurous form of trade, by including chips, eggs, sausages and bacon. These were eaten in any number of combinations each day by people who paid the same attention to their meal as they did the tabloid newspapers. They did not want or expect a great deal.

'The same today, Alex?' The athletic Turkish waiter looked as though he would have been more comfortable on a football ground than swerving between dining tables.

'No, not today, Bulent. No, I think I'd like a whole.' Alisdair, who frequented the café often, was known and liked, although not for his spending capacity because his order usually consisted of only half a kebab. Alisdair was noted for being generous of heart but thrifty of pocket.

'You want a whole shish?' There was a trace of incredulity in the waiter's voice.

'Yes please, and I'll have chips with the salad. Not the rice.'

'Anything else?' The waiter stood before him.

'No, not really,' Alisdair replied ruefully gazing straight at the waiter's ample genitalia which were unavoidably and directly in his line of sight, 'No, I'm afraid that's it.' He sighed and added 'Heigh ho,' mourning for those desires of his life now past.

His meal offered some compensation – as did the glance in the wall mirror. Alisdair had reached that point in a single man's life where he could appreciate himself. This was just as well, he thought, as few others did. The wisps of greying hair that straddled his large balding head, the permanent look of fatigue about his bloodshot eyes, even the blue and purple capillaries (legacies of light and bitter) that decorated his nose – all gave him cause for satisfaction rather than alarm. After all – he had enjoyed his investment.

He thought again of Henry Checket and Peggy Thurston – some strange magnet drew him to their plight. It was not that he felt pity for them. Alisdair was near retiring from the working world himself and unless the world was blown up – he might well be in some kind of home himself. 'God spare us from Veronica Fairhurst – God spare us from . . .' No, Alisdair felt compassion towards Henry and Peggy – he wanted to share their suffering. Past and present, he wished to enter it. He found that he could not eat all his shish kofte and asked the waiter if it might be wrapped up to take home for his cat. This was a strange request as Alisdair's fairly solitary existence did not include animals.

CHAPTER

6

———————

'Now that is very good indeed. I'm pleased with all of you.' Henry and Peggy exchanged puzzled glances. What in God's name could the woman mean? She was very pleased with them? What was good about cutting a potato in two? The woman must be half mad.

They stood with six other residents of Restmore inside the activity room. There were two people to each table – naturally Peggy and Henry were sharing. They both wore aprons, they had been supplied with a pointed cutting knife and a potato. The lady instructor had asked them to cut the potato in half. She moved from one table to another making ecstatic sounds of appreciation and gurgles of encouragement.

Mrs Matherson had taken early retirement at fifty-five from her post of headteacher in an infants school. She sometimes supplemented her pension by doing art and craft sessions with senior citizens groups. As she had remarked to her husband whilst they were on a barge holiday in Worcestershire: 'Most of my life I spent teaching children up to seven years of age and now I'm teaching them over seventy. It doesn't feel all that different.'

Her present group notched up a total of over six hundred years collective experience. Perhaps she was not aware of this. Most of them had worn aprons before and did not need to be shown how to put one on. Certainly, all of them had cut a potato in two. She was unaware of the look of distaste on all their faces. They viewed the potato halves, the paint brushes, the powder paint, the sugar paper, as if some nauseous foreign repast had been set before them.

'When you carve into the face of your potato block – we just want straight cuts. You can have a cross like this. What sort of cross is it?' she enquired brightly.

'A potato cross,' one courteous pupil chose to reply.

'Yes! Yes! It is – And it's also a St George's cross. And this! And this! This is a St Andrew's cross. Anyone here from Scotland?'

This kind of exposition continued for another fifteen minutes before Mrs Matherson allowed her students to commence the baleful activity of making the potato prints. None of the students had any enthusiasm for the task, none of them could see any sense in it whatsoever. Yet, there was another hour to go before teatime – and for the most part, all of the students were quite used to being dutiful.

Henry and Peggy worked slowly. As they worked they talked.

'This is your bloody fault. What are we doing here with this silly cow? We could be in the basement having a cup of tea . . . where did I put those teabags? . . . did I give you the teabags, Henry . . . What a waste of food this is . . .' Peggy did not hide her disgruntlement.

'You know we have to go along with Fairhurst. That's why I put our names on her list. We have to co-operate . . . so far . . . so far.' Henry gouged awkwardly at the potato.

'Suppose you're right. She can't stop us being married? You have told her?'

'I have – I've said it to her.' Henry paused, placed his knife down and added with pride, 'And I've put it in writing. I've put it in writing not just to her . . . but to a higher authority.'

'Not the Queen?'

'No, not as high as that, but high enough.'

'Oh, you are good, Henry. Christ in Heaven, I hate doing this. I think I'll do something else . . . put a bit of sense into it . . .' Peggy flashed her knife adeptly and muttered on.

'Now, I'm going to clap my hands three times. I'll count to each clap. By the end of third clap I want to see your knives out of your hands and on the table. One, Two, Three. There, very, very, very good, not one of you holding your knives.' Mrs Matherson was pleased with her group control. Her class had dropped their knives at 'One', not from respect but from relief.

She placed her hands together as though she were about to pray and spoke in a hushed tone: 'And now, I'm coming round to look at your work. Before you start printing, I want to see your lovely patterns.'

She moved from table to table heaping praise on students who felt either too indifferent or too embarrassed to make a reply. At the last couple's table she said to Henry Checket, 'Mm-mm-that could be effective.' He had gouged out the potato to leave a single raised line.

Her insincere admirations deserted her when she looked over Peggy's shoulder at Peggy's handiwork. Previously, she had bestowed praise as though it were a papal blessing – her tone hushed and reverential.

'Now, what have got here?' There was a harsh timbre to her intonation. 'What have you done with your potato blocks, dear?'

'Eh? What?' Peggy glared at the woman. Was she blind? Couldn't she see what had been done?

'Your blocks? What *have* you done with them?'

'Bloody waste of good food. Potatoes are sixty pence for five pounds. I've made some chips – but they shouldn't be soggy. Got to get the fat right.' Peggy chose not to look at the woman as she spoke. In fact, she had said as much as she was going to say. She had reached a point in life where she rarely spoke to people she did not respect.

The instructor hovered behind Peggy. The rest of the class, sensing some tension, some human drama, were suddenly attentive. Henry, who had often been involved in acts of rescue of one kind or another, patted the back of Peggy's hand with his podgy palm and then placed one of his potato halves before her.

'Now, isn't that kind?' Mrs Matherson moved away from Peggy as she spoke and did not see Henry wince and mutter to Peggy, 'We can eat them later. We can eat the chips later.'

The printing commenced. Henry dipped his potato in green paint and began stamping at the top right hand corner of his sugar paper. He made no attempt at elaborate sequences or patterns. He was making a road. Ought he to give his road a name? He liked looking at the names of roads, lanes and streets. Names flooded into his head . . . Jamaica Road, Crucifix Lane, Tooley Street, Shad, Thames. How could you forget names like that? And how did they just come into your head? Henry pressed on his potato block and was transported to Bermondsey.

The London that Henry found himself in at the beginning of 1946 was not paved with gold. Far from it. What he saw as he walked down Tooley Street was a poor, desolate, devastated area. The man who sold the newspapers had told Henry that the street he was looking for was just off Crucifix Lane. This was Charlie's address – and Henry was convinced that he would find him there. He knew that they had made a mistake about the body. It wasn't Charlie. Charlie could not be dead – he'd be at his home. He'd often told Henry how welcome he'd be in Bermondsey. All Henry had to do now was find the house – he had the number. Yes, it was 23. He found the street, the name was right. Henry caught his breath on first viewing his friend's birthplace.

At one time, the narrow street must have consisted entirely of squat terraced houses. Now it needed some amount of imagination to envisage that much. Great piles of rubble and brick lay on either side of the road where the houses should have stood. Sections of three or four houses were still standing but without roofs. Whole walls were missing leaving partial rooms exposed. It was odd to see the wallpaper of these rooms – their patterns fixed. Perhaps Charlie's family had moved. Henry would have to ask somebody, after all, people in London spoke the same language as him.

It was March and the wind blew dust from the rubble and desolation into Henry's eyes and nose. He squinted and choked. He could see no one. And then, he saw a lady pushing a pram. Has she come from out of the rubble? He crossed the road and walked towards her. It was a nice thought to think that babies were still being born in the middle of all this.

As the woman approached him, he noticed a Union Jack draped on the front of the pram, and underneath it the message, 'Good Luck from Queenie.' Henry felt encouraged by this simple message of goodwill and spoke out as the pram neared him. 'Excuse me, Missus. Excuse me. I wonder if you could help me. I'm looking for a friend.'

'So are we all, dear. So are we all.' In spite of her disparaging tone the woman brought her pram to a halt. Henry realized that she was very thin. She wore a dirty, turquoise turban, a short fur cape that might have been taken from a dead wolf, a flowered frock, and, like most working women or women without wealth, she had orange-coloured legs on account of the sand she had rubbed on them. Stockings were not around for the likes of her. Her face was pale and drawn, most of her teeth were gone and although she was probably about thirty years of age, she looked much older.

Henry thought it might be a good idea to admire her baby. He looked into the pram and his gaze was met by the appealing brown eyes of a mongrel bitch. Henry had not seen a dog in a pram before but expressed no surprise.

'Lovely, ain't she? That's Queenie, that is. That's my little darlin'.' The woman turned her attention to the dog. 'Her's a good gel, then. A good gel, she is. Aren't you a good gel? What yer say you were lookin' for?' She asked this question of her dog but it was addressed to Henry.

'A friend. Charlie Sangster. His family lived in this street. I was a POW with him. I'm back now. He's back. I know he is. I've come to look him up.'

'Well, he's not here. Nor is his family. Yer can see that, can't her. All gone up in smoke with a doodle-bug.'

'A what?'

'A doodle-bug – a rocket. Landed here. What a bleedin' mess. Just when we all thought it was nearly over.' She laughed bitterly. 'No, there weren't no street parties here. Nobody alive to celebrate one. Rotherhithe is worse. I'm leaving the area. Got to spread me wings. No business here.' The woman's last comment seemed to give her some optimism, some sense of purpose. She pointed to the gramophone and the trumpet shaped loudspeaker set up on a platform where the hood of the pram should have been. 'Want to hear a record?'

'A record?' Henry felt sad and empty but he was polite by nature and nurture.

'Yes, a record. You can have Vera Lynn, Ann Shelton, or Dorothy Squires.'

'I'll have the last two.'

'That's a penny each. Twopence.' She held out her hand and Henry gave her a threepenny bit and told her to keep the change.

She wound up the machine and Ann Shelton sang a song entitled 'Praise the Lord and Pass the Ammunition'. As the stirring marching music spilled its melody all about them, Henry could not help thinking, 'God should be very sparing with who He was passing the ammunition to.' Henry did not feel uplifted and made as if to move on.

'Wait a bit. Wait a bit. This one will suit a bit better and you have paid to hear it.' The woman touched his arm and he paused. The record played 'Coming Home My Darling, Coming Home to You'. Henry listened until it had ended. 'That was Dorothy Squires. I hope you find your . . . your . . . friend.' This was 1946 and the woman could say no more. She sensed more, she knew more, but she could not say it. For that matter, neither could Henry. He walked on down the street. If he looked out for all the bands he'd find the saxophone players. Charlie would be, must be, somewhere amongst them. Men like Charlie or Henry didn't have a woman on the side, let alone a man.

He felt someone squeezing his knee. 'She says we can go if we want to.' It was Peggy. She broke into his reverie. If that is what it was. Past and present seemed so close nowadays. He nodded. Peggy removed his apron and as they left the room where only two other students remained she muttered, 'Thank you, dear,' to Mrs Matherson. Mrs Matherson smiled brightly on receiving this comment from such an unexpected source. One could never tell about these things – it had been such a rewarding afternoon.

Peggy and Henry were amongst the last residents of Restmore to enter the large Victorian drawing room. There was usually quite a bit of jostling – and at times – shoving and pushing among the elderly throng as to who should have the best viewing positions for the television. Tea was brought to them on a trolley adeptly trundled between the chairs by a large Filipino lady.

The sense of urgency for position did not match the attention given to any programme once it had been on for a few minutes. In fact, very few people seemed to watch the screen – and yet if someone passed in front of it, there would be murmurs and grumblings. Henry's eyes were riveted to the set. He stared as the blind do – not seeing what was in front of him, but somewhere beyond.

'Drink yer tea – have a sip.' Peggy passed him a cup. 'And here, here, I saved you a digestive.' She plucked a biscuit from inside her brassière which now served as a secret pocket. The brassière was no longer a garment of privacy, mystery, or eroticism.

Henry turned unseeing eyes towards her, received his tea and smiled as he spoke to Peggy.

'Thank you, Charlie. Thank you, mate. D'you know? D'you know, Charlie – I'd forgotten what you looked like. After all this time – I'd forgot. I am happy. Oh, Charlie.'

Peggy had always liked nick-names and was pleased to hear this new one Henry had conferred on her. Nothing about Henry could cause her any irritation. He was such a comfort. Someone belched loudly.

'What was that?' Henry asked of her.

'A bit of wind. Someone's got a bit of wind. That's all – eat your biscuit and drink your tea. Don't worry yer head over a bit of wind.'

'Sounded like a trombone,' said Henry.

CHAPTER

7

———————

24 Botswana Road
Bounds Green
London N22

Dear Mr McClennon,

Thank you for your interesting letter. I have not returned
to social work since leaving my position in order to
take maternity leave. We had not expected twins as there was
no previous history of multiple birth in either my husband's
family or mine. Also, much to my surprise, I managed
to produce a baby girl only eleven months after my two boys
were born. I now have three children under three and
propose to regulate my fecundity for the foreseeable future!!

I would be more than happy to discuss Peggy Thurston
with you. She was one of my last clients and she, above all
others, will always remain indelibly imprinted on my mind.

Due to my present domestic circumstances it is quite
difficult for me to travel – and I don't see how I can get up
to your office during working hours. However, if you should
wish to call here, I should be happy to see you. Afternoons
– between 2.30 and 4.00 are the best times – as (if I'm
lucky) the children have a nap then.

Yours sincerely,

Jane Mumbry (Ms)

Alisdair McClennon did not feel guilty about ringing Jane Mumbry's bell with prolonged insistence. It was two-thirty precisely – but Alisdair knew that if her children could sleep through the pneumatic drill pounding on the road outside her house, then they could sleep through anything.

He was greeted by an attractive, comfortable-looking woman in her late thirties. Although the day was chill with an air of expectant frost, Jane Mumbry wore a cotton frock with a shirt-like neckline, patterned with tiny red and orange roses. Her brow was wide and she had large, soft, brown eyes. Her appearance was slightly odd or eccentric. 'It must be her hair,' he thought. Not that brunettes were unusual – but Jane Mumbry must have only applied a brush and added two plastic bands by way of coiffure. Her shoulder-length hair was simply parted down the middle and bunched into *two* pony tails. One hung either side of her face. It gave her the presence of an appealing spaniel.

'Alisdair McClennon? Do come in.' Alisdair lip-read Jane Mumbry's invitation. The noise from the road seemed louder. He followed her through the hall.

'I hope you don't mind sitting in the kitchen,' she called over her shoulder, 'only we have dry rot in the floor boards in the lounge and it's just been treated.'

They settled quickly and Alisdair opened the conversation apologetically. 'It's very good of you to see me like this, on a Saturday. I hope I'm not keeping you from too many other things. Your children . . .'

'They're asleep now. They'll be in noddyland for at least a couple of hours. My husband works on Saturday.'

'Oh?' Alisdair's facial expression asked the question.

'He's the manager of a betting shop. Did a degree in fine arts.' She shrugged; her pony tails twitched. 'But we have a mortgage . . . and . . . and he likes the job.'

'Good, I'm glad.' Alisdair wondered why certain jobs always carried apologetic addenda. 'I've come to talk about Mrs Peggy Thurston – or at least, I've come to hear you talk about Mrs Thurston.'

'Do you like her?' Jane Mumbry asked.

'Yes. Did you?' He answered in the same direct tone.

'I adored her,' Jane replied pensively. 'Perhaps we can both talk about her. You tell me what is relevant to the present, and I'll tell you the same about the past.'

'She was one of your favourite clients?'

'It was her friend, Miss Lamb, who was my client, not Mrs Thurston. Miss Lamb had been referred to us by her GP. He was concerned about Miss Lamb's physical health which he felt was deteriorating because of what he termed "certain oddities" in her social behaviour.'

'These oddities of behaviour . . . ?'

'There were none. None at all.' Jane Mumbry shook her head as she spoke. 'It was just . . . it was just . . . charity.'

'Ah, there are many today who would consider that odd. These are harsh times.' Alisdair's voice suddenly became infected with a Scots burr. Jane continued, encouraged by his response.

'Both women were in their seventies when I knew them. They lived in Islington – not the fashionable part. They lived not far from the Arsenal football stadium. Sometimes, if I visited them at their terraced home I could hear the roar of the crowds coming from the ground. Miss Lamb was saddened that such enthusiasm could not be put to better use. I must admit the arena at Rome couldn't have sounded much more intimidating. Not that anything would have frightened Miss Lamb or Mrs Thurston.'

'Why do you say that?'

'There are not many women of seventy or over who would chance their arm walking the streets of London in the early hours of the morning. Most women, whatever their age, would be in fear, or at least, very apprehensive.'

'I agree with you – women who did such a thing could be considered in hazard, at risk, immoral . . .' Alisdair paused and looked questioningly at Jane, '. . . or even a little mad?'

'They were quite sane. Two or three times a week, they ventured forth. Each pushed one of those supermarket trolleys. If either of them had ever been accosted, there was little that could be plundered. The trolleys held any number of cheese or spam rolls and also flasks of hot soup. They knew all the spots within a three mile radius where they would find human beings that church and state had given up on. People who had given up on themselves.'

'Perhaps we all do that from time to time, Mrs Mumbry.'

'Only to a degree; I'd rather you not make comments as though this was some form of analysis.'

Alisdair laughed. 'I was wondering to myself – I'm sorry. I'll try not to do it again.' He liked this woman. He had noticed wet patches about the peaks of Jane's breasts. Was she still feeding the baby? 'How did you know of these journeys – these sorties into the night?'

'I accompanied them once or twice. They did Euston, King's Cross, Camden Town, Finsbury Park, Clerkenwell. They were known to their parishioners, although they never mentioned God, Christ, Goodness, Salvation or anything like that. They just gave out the hot drink and food and said little.'

'What were they known as? Nomenclatures always fascinate me.'

'Mum and Dad.'

'Good Lord! How odd.'

'Well, you see, Miss Lamb had a somewhat masculine appearance. I'm sure that even the most far gone alcoholics would have been aware of her sex – but for some reason they gave her another gender completely. A masculine one. She said herself that she had a man's mind in a woman's body. I never corrected her.'

'The best might be a combination of the two. The masculine and the feminine. They sound like a remarkable duo.'

'Oh, they were. Convention meant little to them. This is why Miss Lamb was referred to me. She was not bounded by convention. Neighbours had complained about the cats.'

'Cats?'

'They had seven – and they fed strays.' Jane laughed. 'It's not difficult to meet the needy in any form, is it? If you are available they find you.'

'Did you know much about their backgrounds – what had gone on before you knew them?'

'Quite a bit,' Jane answered cautiously. 'They met during the war. Both were engaged in farm work. Their social backgrounds were dissimilar. Miss Lamb was the only child of a vicar, and Mrs Thurston was from a poor working class family. Mrs Thurston's husband was away soldiering at the time. Then they both lost track of one another – for many years. In fact, they did not meet again until two days before Mrs Thurston's fifty-second birthday.'

'But how did they . . . who wrote . . . ?'

'The meeting was quite accidental. Miss Lamb found Peggy Thurston in the doorway of a shop near Euston. She had already started to distribute food alone, before Mrs Thurston joined her.'

'Mrs Thurston was a vagrant, then?'

'I wouldn't put it that way. She was adrift. Peggy told me this herself. It was not revealed by Miss Lamb. From my visits it seemed as though the two of them had spent a lifetime together. In spite of the cats, the odd people calling to scrounge food, there was a great deal of harmony in their home.'

'And relatives?'

'Miss Lamb had none. Her mother she had barely known and she referred to her dead father without affection. "If my father is in heaven, then I hope that there are no other people there. He could not understand anyone remotely different from himself." Miss Lamb read a great deal. There were great piles of books stacked everywhere. I'm sorry, I haven't even offered you a cup of tea.'

Alisdair raised his hand. 'No, no, not unless you're having one yourself.' He leaned forward. Jane was aware of his urgency. 'And Mrs Thurston's relatives?'

'Why do you want to know? Why?' Her question was muttered.

'Mrs Thurston needs help.'

'Too vague. Don't we all need it?'

'Er . . . er . . . she wishes to marry. Is she free to marry?'

'Yes.'

'But . . . er . . . her husband?'

'He's dead.'

'You're quite sure? I have to be absolutely cer. . .'

Jane cut in. 'He died in prison in 1969. After he'd served three years of a seven year sentence.'

'I thought sentencing was lenient in those days.'

'It was lenient. Very lenient. The charge was manslaughter. He had killed the woman he was living with. When murders are committed at home the elevated state of the "family" always gives such enormous leeway. You must know this. "Domestic" quarrels, somehow, allow for bodily harm. I can remember it exactly: "Mr Thurston during a domestic quarrel had punched his common-law wife about the head and throat. He had then proceeded to kick her about the stomach and groin. She died of internal injuries." He pleaded manslaughter on the grounds of drink and provocation – there had been no intent to kill.' Jane laughed bitterly. 'He had apparently also declared that he had fought in the war, that he was sorry, and that he had become a born again Christian. His plea of manslaughter was accepted.'

'But you don't think it was manslaughter?'

'I'm not a judge. But I'm not sorry he's dead. So you see Peggy is free to marry. I found this out after Miss Lamb died. Just in case Peggy might need it.'

'Peggy – Mrs Thurston . . . she was very upset . . . at Miss Lamb's death?'

'Yes, but she accepted it calmly. She said Miss Lamb had died like Mrs Gaskell.'

'Who?'

'Mrs Gaskell, a novelist. A Victorian novelist, a contemporary of Dickens. Miss Lamb was very fond of her work. Apparently, she was reading aloud to Peggy when she died. It was late afternoon. Peggy was listening. It was a story entitled "Bliss", by Katherine Mansfield. Half way through a sentence Miss Lamb had gasped, winced, and then her head had fallen forward onto her chest. A quick death – with little premonition.'

'I suppose Mrs Thurston deteriorated after this?'

'No, no, not at all. She gave away most of the money Miss Lamb had left her to charities. Peggy was most accountable. She found homes for all the cats. Cleaned up the house. Put the place up for sale. Then delivered me an ultimatum.'

'What was that?'

'"Put me in a home, Jane. Put me in a home."' Jane mimicked Peggy. '"If you don't, I'll take my chances back on the street again. I could do worse. The streets might be better. It's all the luck of the draw. I won't stay here, though. Not without Larry."'

'You haven't mentioned him before.'

'I have. Larry was Peggy's nickname for Miss Lamb.'

'Oh! Oh!' Alisdair's exclamations were tinged with regret. 'And this man – this man that Peggy wants to marry. Do you like him, Mr McClennon? Will he be good to Peggy?'

'I like the sound of him. And if . . . but we cannot plot other people's destinies, Mrs Mumbry.' He stood. 'I've taken up a lot of your time. You have been very helpful. I'll let you know how things go.'

Jane remained seated. She would not show him to the door, not yet. 'Is Mrs Thurston happy at Restmore?'

'Not unhappy. There are some problems. Personality conflicts, you know.'

'No, I don't know. I am asking.'

Alisdair drew on his gloves. 'Our officer-in-charge – Mrs Fairhurst . . . er . . . Mrs Thurston and her fiancé, Mr Checket – neither of them is too keen on her.'

'Neither was I. I thought she was a right b. . .'

'Ahem,' Alisdair cleared his throat, 'well, I'll leave you now. Is that one of your children I can hear?'

'Yes – feeding time. I'm a walking milkbar.' Jane saw him to the door. 'What about you? Do you like Veronica Fairhurst?'

The roar of the pneumatic drill obliterated his answer. This was just as well as his response had been less than professional.

CHAPTER
8

Peggy had said to Henry that they ought to spend more time in each other's room. It would help them become more used to each other and to sort out their separate space later on. This meant that Peggy would spend more time in his room. Her own room was inspected by the staff too often, whereas Henry, for the most part, was left alone.

It was 9.30 p.m. Peggy had said that she would just like to collect a few of her own things to put in his room – she had referred to them 'as just a few bits of comfort'. Henry was beginning to feel some concern. Peggy had been gone for almost an hour. It ought not to take her so long to collect a few bits. There were other fears. When he married Peggy, would they have to share a room? And if they did, would he have to share . . . ? Oh, God . . . he'd never done that with anybody, not a whole night. Henry had only really been familiar with the perimeters of his own body for most of his life.

The tap, tap on his door put such thoughts from his head. He was not surprised to see Peggy. After all, he had been expecting her. But what was she doing coming in with this great plastic bag slung over her shoulder? She looked like one of the peasant women he had seen working in Siam. Was she leaving the home? Had she come to say goodbye?

'There!' With a loud sigh Peggy plonked the bag on the floor near his cubicle. 'Don't stand there gawping, Henry. Close the door. You know what this place is like. It's about as private as Mae

West's knickers.' She sat on the floor next to the bag and rested her back against the wall. Henry had observed that Peggy could make herself comfortable anywhere, with or without furniture. He closed the door, sat on his bed, and watched Peggy rummage in her bag.

'Ah, there it is.' She took out an envelope. From the envelope she extracted what looked like two photographs. 'Like to see them? I have to have these on the wall.' She proffered one to Henry. It was faded and in dark brown and white. But the picture was clear enough. A lady in jodhpurs and a check shirt was leaning on a spade. She had short hair and a square jaw and she stood like a farm worker. But she must have been a lady on account of her large breasts. 'That's Larry,' Peggy said simply but with affection. 'My golden girl. Here,' she passed him the other card. Henry looked at this longer. It was a picture in full colour of a man wearing foreign clothes. He was very handsome. Dark brown eyes, a full mouth and . . . Henry turned the picture over, curious about a possible message on the back. Past endearments, past affections, passions, loves . . .

Henry frowned. There was no message. But printed on the bottom it said: A Young Man. Antello da Messina. Active – 1456. Died 1479. The National Gallery. Henry's eyes asked Peggy the question.

'I met him during the war. Italian. Prisoner of War. Oh, he was lovely. I didn't know whether I was on my arse or my elbow with him, I can tell you. Thought my head was going to fall off with all his loving.' She shook her head. 'No more . . . no more, after him. Not any that counted. Two that forced themselves on me while I was on the road. Horrible. As for that creature I married . . . I never saw Valerio again after the prisoners were sent away. That's him. That's Valerio.'

Henry looked at the dates. He was no great shakes at arithmetic but even he could see that Peggy must be very, very old if she knew this man. She must be ancient.

'I found it inside a book. In this place, too, somebody had used it as a marker. Fancy, after all these years, finding a picture of him in here.' She peered into her bag. 'There's some sellotape somewhere.'

'You were lucky,' said Henry. 'He looks very nice. I can understand you liking him.' And then he lied. 'He might still be alive somewhere – and perhaps he might have found a picture of you. Just as you were. You never know, do you?'

Peggy did not answer his question. Her young man had entered history once more. 'There. Put that on your table. It's run on batteries. You don't have to plug it in.' She handed him a small transistor radio. This was followed by a chipped mug with 'LMS' printed on it, a book called *Sylvia's Lovers* by Mrs Gaskell, and an egg-timer. 'That's nearly all of it.' Peggy leaned back and folded her arms.

Henry was puzzled. She had unloaded precious little. He could easily accommodate these few extra effects in his room. The bag still looked full. Where was Peggy taking the rest of her things? He yawned heavily and then covered his mouth quickly with his hand. He did not want Peggy to witness his fatigue. But how much longer was she going to stay? This thought added to his confusions as he had begun to realise that when she was absent he missed her. Apart from Charlie, he had never sought or wanted much company.

'What time are you turning in, then?' she asked. She had noticed his yawn.

'Soon, I think.'

'Well, don't mind me, then. When you're ready – get between the sheets.' Peggy stood, turned from him and began to tug at something inside the plastic bag. She spoke through her industry. 'Switch the wireless on, Henry. It's "Book at Bedtime". I like to be read to. It's a book about India again. One in every three is about India. The way posh people lived there and how some were upset on account of having to leave and some were upset at having to stay. Either way, I'm getting a bit fed up of them. There's nice bits of music, though, in between the readings. Indian music it is.'

'Never heard any.' Henry twiddled with the dials.

'Sounds like violins playing under water ... Lovely. Ah!

There, that's it.' Peggy's exclamation of achievement brought Henry's attention from the radio to her. He smiled with a mixture of pleasure and relief as he watched her shake a dark brown, nylon sleeping bag. She unzipped the bag, fetched a cushion from the chair, placed it at the base of the cubicle and spread the bag down in front of it. Then she began to undress.

'Will you be comfortab!ɔ?' Henry spoke to a background of sitar music.

'Wouldn't be comfortable anywhere else. Slept on the floor for years. I hate soft beds. Give me back ache. Waste of laundry ever changing the sheets on my bed. I've never slept there.' Peggy was half undressed. She did not seemed shy or demure about taking her clothes off in front of Henry. He thought that it might be as well to get used to this state of affairs and began to do the same.

They arrived at nakedness about the same time. While Henry began to put on his pyjamas and Peggy squirmed into a night-dress, Peggy said, 'Your breasts are bigger than mine, Henry.' Henry could see that Peggy's hair was thinner than his. He thought that, as men and women got older, they began to look more alike. Bits that had previously stuck out had now shrunk. In some ways it was like being a child again.

He watched Peggy zip herself up for the night. He pulled the sheets over his own body and switched off the light. The sitars had stopped crooning and the voice on the radio was telling them how faithful this Indian servant had been and . . .

Servant, Servant. Do this. Do that. Now, when you've finished . . . You forgot . . . Don't put the . . . Remember to . . . In by eight . . . Free on Sunday afternoon . . . Get your meals from . . . I expect . . . Servant . . . servant. Service. Peggy, half asleep, half awake was there again.

'You're a lucky girl,' her mother had said. It was just two days after Peggy's thirteenth birthday. 'A lucky girl. There's a clean set of everything.' She snapped the small case shut. 'It's not every girl gets a place in service. See that you send your wages home. I've not kept you all these years for nothing. And there's more than enough mouths to feed here. I'll see you to the train. Here let me look at you.'

Peggy felt she should have been excited as she stood with her mother and waited for the train's arrival. She had seen a train but never travelled on one. Now, she was bound for Birmingham, a big city. A label was attached to the lapel of her coat stating who she was. At Birmingham, New Street Station, she was to be collected by the people who were to be her employers. Peggy felt as though she had been sold rather than employed. She couldn't leave even if she wanted to. 'Don't come running home squawk-arsing or you'll be sent straight back. Places don't grow on trees,' her mother said as the train snorted and belched its way into the station. Peggy had not realised trains were so noisy. Her mother left the platform before the train pulled out.

Through the carriage window she had watched her only known environment fly past. Farming and coalmining were of the land, the earth. One was conducted on top of it – and the other beneath. The deserted pitbanks looked so beautiful at this time of the year. She caught a glimpse of grey earth patchworked with pink willow-herb and yellow coltsfoot, and pools surrounded by bullrush and wild iris. She put her head out of the window to see and sniff it all. A spark had entered her eye, steam and smoke had choked her nostrils. It was all over – childhood ended earlier if you were poor.

Although Peggy's new residence was in Birmingham she never actually saw the city. She had been collected at the station and taken straight to Edgbaston by Mrs Roker who told her, 'Now, when you get home again, Peggy, don't tell people that you are in Birmingham. Tell them that you are in Edgbaston. Do remember.' Peggy nodded, knowing she would say nothing at all. Mainly because nobody would be particularly interested. Mrs Roker's husband was 'in business'. Her mistress used this phrase herself as though it were hallowed in some way.

For three years, Peggy was daily informed of how fortunate and privileged she was to serve. Peggy rose at five a.m. to clean grates and light fires. Household tasks of one kind or another were not difficult to come by. There was scrubbing, polishing, ironing, washing, mending ... It never stopped and Mrs Roker always managed to say that Peggy was behind with this or that ... At nine p.m. Peggy was glad to be in bed – sleep was her greatest luxury throughout this period.

She travelled home every four months. This was called her four day leave. Her mother used to count the halfcrowns before Peggy had taken off her coat. It was on the station that she met her future husband. They had exchanged very few sentences. He had proposed on her next journey. His mother had died. He had a small house. He needed a woman. Peggy's following visit home, she had married him at the registry office. She was seventeen, then, and felt that after Mrs Roker she could only go forward.

Peggy had quickly realised that she had merely left one kind of service to enter another. She was dutiful and did obey her husband, but after three weeks of marriage there was not the smallest recess in her heart that honoured him. Service ... service ... 'You there, Larry? ... You there, Larry ... ?' she mumbled drowsily, chloroformed by sleep.

'Yes, just about, Charlie ... just about,' Henry replied.

He was in a long room – there were twelve beds. 'Lights out. Eyes shut. Time to sleep, now.' It seemed a daft thing to say. There were no lights on. The room was flooded with daylight. The thin curtains had been drawn across the windows – but it was still bright and there were noises of people outside, not sleeping.

'No talking. No chatter, now. It's Bedfordshire time.' The matron stamped past each boy, checking that all eyes were closed. It was a warm evening in June. It was seven p.m. and that was bedtime. An orphanage, like a school or a prison, was dependent on a great deal of routine and ritual if it was to maintain a sense of order. Henry had not been a lad for breaking rules. Perhaps this was why he had been granted this second childhood.

'A quiet youth of no particular skill, charm, or ability. Tends to live very much in a world of his own.' That was the final sentence passed on Henry when he was catapulted from the orphanage into the working world. But if the world that you knew was very painful – wouldn't you invent a private one for yourself?

The reading had stopped. The music had started again. He was with Peggy. In India, was it? He called out. He called out in a loud, odd voice, a voice that did not seem to belong to him.

'I love you, Peggy. I've loved you, perhaps from even before I was born.'

'What time is it? Breakfast time, is it?' Peggy struggled for words, scratching her head.

'No, no. It's still night.' Henry was embarrassed.

'Henry, when we are married, don't wake me up to tell me something I already know.'

CHAPTER
9

The armchair was perfectly placed; in hastening to sit on it Alisdair knocked a potted plant off a coffee table onto the carpet. He retrieved it quickly and replaced it. He had always been clumsy and his sense of direction was poor, which he had realised ever since his national service days. He hoped that he had not gained too much attention as he sank into the chair.

It was visitors' time at Restmore. Nobody had appeared to notice his mishap – even him for that matter. Immediately to his right a family sat hunched round a small, circular coffee table, and talked without looking at one another – their eyes focused on the television. Alisdair looked at them – three generations.

The old man's hand shook as he spoke and he had to grip the inside of his armchair to stop the hand leaving it of its own free will. It certainly belonged to him but it acted as though it were driven by some other force and wished to escape. His daughter, dressed in a light green woollen twinset, frowned often. Her brows seemed set on contradicting whatever her father had to say. Her own daughter's visit to her grandfather was negated by the headphones around her ears as she swayed her head from side to side mentally drugging herself with the latest pop mixture.

Alisdair wondered if this young girl's appearance might shock some of the elderly – but they seemed as indifferent to this young lady with white face make-up, two rings in her nose and black-red lips, as she was to them. Her hair sprouted from her head in heavily lacquered pale-green spikes. She might have arrived to perform the Dance of Death. She chewed gum whilst her mother and grandfather talked.

'Ah, that's Charlton Heston. Seen him in lots of films. *Ben Hur*, Bible films, that sort of thing,' the old man observed as he viewed the television.

'No, dad, no, it's not.' His daughter's frown deepened. It's not Charlton Heston. It's the pope. This is the news. That's the pope climbing down from an aeroplane and kissing the ground. It's not Charlton Heston.'

The old man grunted. 'Pope my arse, it's Charlton Heston. He's an actor.' More news continued.

'There you are . . . I told you. Murders on the Thames . . . bank fraud . . .' The daughter sighed, looked at her watch and muttered, 'He's impossible,' and tapped her own daughter on the knee, 'time to go'. They both rose and brushed the old man's bald pate with their lips. He took no notice of this demonstration of duty and did not turn his gaze to them as they left him.

As Alisdair watched, Peggy and Henry entered – Peggy led Henry as though he were some tired old labrador. They sat in the chairs next to him, immediately to the left of the dark-blue curtain. From where they were sitting they could not see the television.

'Poor girl . . .' Peggy commented on the young girl that she had seen leave. 'Something must have frightened her when she was young. Must have been horrible, to do that to her hair. Fright can give you terrible things – she's deaf as well. Aids on both ears.' Alisdair watched them settle into their chairs.

Henry sat and looked out of the windows. Eyes open, mind dreaming. His dream was filled with sparkling lights in darkened places. Bits of eyes, ears, thighs, tits, bums lit up and moved this way and that. He sniffed the scents of *Evening in Paris*, *June* and *Californian Poppy*. This was a waltz. Where was he? The Tower Ballroom at Blackpool? The Rialto at Scarborough? The Co-op Hall at Cannock. The Bouverie Ballroom at Stoke Newington . . . ? The huge mirrored ball spun round and the dancers took the floor. At these times, Henry scrutinised the sax section of the bands. He never saw the face he searched for. There were many towns. Couldn't count them all. Not difficult to get a job. Porter, hospital porter, kitchen porter. Porter, hotel porter, kitchen porter . . . 'Those bright lights in the ballroom . . . sometimes they made me feel naked when they shone on me. I used to dodge about to try to miss them – but they'd always settle on you.'

'Oh, Henry, you wouldn't want to be caught naked, would you?' Peggy patted his hand and chuckled.

'No, oh no, I wouldn't. I would risk anything . . .'

'I was naked. As naked as I was when I was brought into the world. It was the second time with that Valerio. And he took every stitch of clothing off me. In broad daylight. "Look at me. Look," he said. I couldn't bring myself to at first but with his urging . . . I did. We never had the freedom or the licence to do with each other what we did . . .'

'"No, Charlie, not here," I said. "They'll kill us if they see us . . . the guards will kill us." He pulled me on to my knees before him. "Come on . . . help me, Henry. Help me out. It won't take a couple of minutes. Yer know yer love me . . . come on." He never seemed to notice how hard it was raining . . . So I did what he asked me to and I didn't feel bad about it. It wasn't only our rice we shared. I hate rice pudding – can't touch rice now.'

'Rice pudding. We never had rice pudding today, Henry. It was jam roll. You liked it. You even ate a bit of mine that I left over.'

'Did I, Peggy? It was greedy of me if I did.'

'You know you did. Oh, you are a caution. I wonder if they are coming round with the tea trolley?'

Alisdair chose his moment. 'I'll get a cup for you. Two teas, is it? And sugar in both?' He stood and moved his chair closer to them as he spoke.

'Yes, dear, thank you . . . We've both got a sweet tooth. Not that we can call out teeth our own. Yes, please, one cup for me and one for my fiancé. Peggy's response was quick and sharp. As Alisdair went to collect the tea she muttered behind her hand to Henry. 'Who's he? One of Fairhurst's spies?'

'I'm Alisdair McClennon.' An introduction was needed. Henry

nodded but did not speak. Peggy stirred her tea noisily and then in a short staccato fashion said, 'I'm Peggy Thurston and he's Henry – Henry Checket.'

'Pleased to meet you,' Alisdair answered quietly.

'We're going to be married.' Peggy's statement was made in the tone of an edict or declaration.

'Yes, I know,' Alisdair said.

'Oh, do you?' Henry's torpor had been jolted. He was aware when he needed to be.

'Did you read it in the papers? Funny, that is – as we've only told people that live here. We've no world outside. No one close to us. Not living, anyway. Do you have relations here? Or are you coming to live here?' Peggy enquired.

'He's not old enough,' said Henry.

'Might have gone a bit off in the head early. Some do – get old before they're due to and . . .' Peggy's conjectures were cut short by Alisdair.

'I'm a colleague of Mrs Fairhurst.'

'Eh? What?' The elderly couple questioned in unison.

'Mrs Fairhurst. I'm her superior.'

'That's not difficult,' Peggy snapped. 'So am I. Better than her – la-da-da-di, simper, simper any day of any week . . .'

'No! I mean – I'm her boss.'

'She takes her orders from you, does she?' Henry asked now in unbelieving fashion.

'Not exactly. But . . . but . . . she is accountable to me.'

'You mean, she couldn't kick us out of here without your say-so. She couldn't dump us away as if we were a pair of dumbos.' Peggy turned to Henry. 'You hear that, Henry?'

'You could stop her, then – you could stop her – if she wanted to put us away? Henry was as persistent as Peggy had been. Alisdair was entranced by their joint tenacity.

'I would have to agree,' Alisdair said.

'Do you know much about us?' Peggy asked.

'Quite a bit,' said Alisdair.

'Your life's not your own,' Henry ruminated aloud. 'What's

gone doesn't even belong to you and what's to come seems to be worked out already by others. We never asked you to talk to us. Why? Why? What are you doing with us two here? Fetching our tea, and asking how much sugar we want?'

'I want to help,' replied Alisdair somewhat sadly.

Peggy felt that Alisdair meant what he said, and in spite of her innate distrust of people who worked in any institution decided to be generous. 'You're not from London, are you?'

'No, I'm not. I was born in Scotland.' Alisdair was grateful to Peggy for reducing the tension.

'Lovely scenery there,' Henry observed emptily and without enthusiasm.

'Not where I was born. All my family were coalminers. Coal-cutters. I was the odd one out.' Alisdair hunched his shoulders and opened his hands as though he expected some sympathy for being different.

'I can see that they're not working hands.' Peggy held out her own hands and turned them this way and that. 'Look at mine. Dear God, you'd think they belonged to a man – but not when I was young. Then, if you had hands like mine you were a woman and you worked. If they were like yours you were a lady and you didn't work.'

'I like your hands, Peggy,' Henry commiserated. 'I like rough hands. The touch of smooth hands gives me the creeps.'

Alisdair was about to suggest that the three of them might take a walk when he felt a tap on his shoulder. Before turning he noticed that both Peggy and Henry seemed intent on studying kneecaps. They stared with heads bowed.

'Ah, there you are, Mr McClennon, I've been searching for you.' Veronica Fairhurst used much the same tone to everyone when she was on home ground. 'I wonder if you could spare me a few moments. Of course, I hate to drag you away.' She waited for a response or for him to stand and then follow her. He did neither. He turned about to face Henry and Peggy and remained seated.

'Ahem! Ahem! Mr McClennon, are you going to . . .'

'No, no, not at the moment – I'll join you in fifteen or twenty minutes. If you're not free, I'll call in during the week.'

'Very well.' Veronica Fairhurst left the lounge with as much dignity as she could muster.

Peggy laughed and cackled. She nudged Henry who smiled. 'That's one in the eye for bossy-drawers. Didn't expect that, did she? No, she did not. It's got to be "No, Mrs Fairhurst, yes, Mrs Fairhurst, thank you very much, Mrs Fairhurst, three bags full, Mrs Fairhurst."'

'He's a friend, Peggy. This man's our friend,' said Henry.

'What were you tellin' us – before Madam arrived?' Peggy asked Alisdair. He scratched his head. What had he been saying?

'Do you know, I've completely forgotten.' He laughed lightly. 'It's quite gone from my mind.'

'You're getting like us,' said Henry.

'That's not so bad a thing,' Peggy added.

'No, no, I suppose not. I suppose you're right,' said Alisdair.

A few days later Veronica Fairhurst greeted Alisdair in her office with much concern and effusion. 'You must feel quite drained. I'll ring down for some tea. I know only too well how wearing those two can be.'

'No, no tea, thank you. I had some earlier. I took it in the lounge. I've been talking to your care staff. They are a very impressive group. So much insight and so hardworking.' Alisdair sighed. 'I only wish we could pay them more.'

'Ah, money is not everything, Mr McClennon, I'm sure my women get a lot of satisfaction from what they do.'

'Yes, I agree – they must – or they wouldn't work so hard for such a slender wage. Oh, at least three of them mentioned that there is a great improvement in Mrs Thurston and Mr Checket. You must be pleased.'

'I would be pleased if it were true. I think they are being dangerously sentimental. Sometimes non-professionals do let their hearts govern their heads – often with disastrous consequences. I'm sure you know this – if only they could marry the two – the heart and the head. But we cannot expect too much from the ordinary.'

'Marry?' Alisdair seized on the word.

'Ah, you have heard.' Mrs Fairhurst laughed aloud so that the pearl necklace about her throat wobbled. Alisdair felt that he might like to tighten the necklace. She patted away imaginary tears from her eyes with a tiny embroidered handkerchief. 'One shouldn't laugh –but then farce and tragedy are perilously close, don't you think?' She gave him no time to answer this question.

She had leaned forward on her desk, arms outstretched, hands clenched, so that the knuckles shone white. 'And tragedy it would be, Mr McClennon, if this episode should ever take place. I will not call it marriage.'

'If the church or state validated it, then it would be a marriage, Mrs Fairhurst. Such an office is not in our hands to exercise.'

'It would be like allowing children to marry.'

'Mrs Thurston and Mr Checket are not children, Mrs Fairhurst. Maturity does not always come with age and I do feel . . .'

'A marriage between those two will not take place here . . . It is *their* welfare I am thinking of. I mean . . . had . . . you . . . had you considered the nitty gritty side of marriage, Mr McClennon?'

'Nitty gritty?' Lord, what in God's name was this woman thinking up now, Alisdair thought. He watched her place the handkerchief in the top drawer of her desk. For some reason she took out some spectacles with large round rims. She placed them on her face and blinked at him like some great owl. He waited for the wisdom.

'I hate to personalise things, but I ask you, Mr McClennon, how would your wife feel if you had never consummated your marriage?' Here she raised a hand and pointed towards him with her index finger. ' . . . or, what if your wife had not agreed to consummation – how would you feel?'

'The question is not personalised. I am not married.'

'Oh dear, oh dear . . .' Mrs Fairhurst murmured with mock regret. She was of that increasing body of men and women who believed that anyone who remained single was probably homosexual. She was absolutely convinced about this. The absurdity of such a notion never entered her mind. For her the single status indicated a personality defect. She was a tidy woman who wished to have tidy marriages. 'Well, I do speak here from personal experience of these things . . . It's rather delicate . . . How can I put it . . . er'm . . . It would not be in Mr Checket's nature to be able to consummate the . . . Do you understand me, Mr McClennon?'

'Yes, I'm sure I do . . . but isn't Mr Checket capable of loving. Is love without sex meaningless? If we are personalising this matter, and it would seem at this point it is unavoidable, if I were to marry – I could marry for love without sex. I could not marry for sex without love.' Alisdair shook his head.

Veronica Fairhurst was pleased to see her senior unnerved. Why did he wear a ring on his wedding finger if he was a bachelor? A bachelor gay? Was there anyone who might be able to tell her? And if she knew for sure, was there anything she could do with such knowledge?

'A true marriage is declared void without . . . nuptials, Mr McClennon. It is not merely some romantic arrangement.'

'You're right, Mrs Fairhurst. It is, however, left to one of the two partners to make such a declaration, you know.'

'But, Mr McClennon! You have met these two . . . Can you imagine . . .'

'I never try to imagine what my married friends do in bed. That is a matter wholly and entirely of their concern. If they do nothing, then that, too, is their business.'

Veronica waved her hand in front of her face as though someone had puffed fumes of smoke before her eyes. 'Very well. Then, I wonder if you would mind having a look at this recent medical report on Mrs Thurston. There's a small matter of incontinence that we might have to . . .'

Alisdair got up from his chair and stood next to her as she opened out the file. He leaned forward – and she swayed to the right so as to be as far away from him as possible. Garlic! He had eaten a double houmus that lunchtime and his pores oozed the smell of it. He was glad that she found his odour objectionable, and paused over the notes longer than necessary. Alisdair did have this spiteful side to his nature but chose to use it sparingly.

'Finished yer tea, dear?' Peggy enquired of Henry.

'Yes, I was thinking.'

'Well, you do a lot of that. Our minds aren't our own, are they? Nor our bodies, sometimes.'

'Eh, what's that, Peggy?'

'I said, "our bodies". I don't think we can get married, Henry.'

'Oh, why?'

'Well, it's my body. It's that . . .'

'I thought we'd settled all that. All that about bed and . . .'

'Oh, no love, no, no, it's not that. Not worried about *that*. It's just that sometimes, Henry, sometimes . . . I wet myself.'

'Oh, is that all. I know about that.'

'But what if I did it . . . when we shared full time?'

'I'd clean it up. Or we'd clean it up. Simple as that.'

'Henry, I love you.'

'Oh, I know. And I'm not complaining. They've drawn the curtains already.' Henry deftly changed the subject.

'Dark outside. Gets dark outside early now. I don't know why they've drawn the curtains, though. It's not as though there is a war on, is it?'

'No, it's not,' said Henry.

Alisdair felt that if he lingered near Veronica Fairhurst's side long enough, she might well fall off her chair. Her face which was usually of a freshly scrubbed hue had changed and she looked pale. He closed the file on the desk. 'I don't think this is too much of a problem. Intermittent enuresis is not uncommon here, is it?' He moved from her side and stood and gazed out of the window as he asked his question.

'No, no, it's not. It might be in marriage, though. I speak from experience.'

'Oh, do you or your husband suffer from it?' He still considered the view, not her face, as he talked.

'Certainly not. I think you misunderstood my meaning.'

'I'm sorry, Mrs Fairhurst.' Alisdair looked about him. 'My overcoat – ah – it's downstairs. I remember, now. I left it in the hallway. I'll pop in again. Informally, same as before – if you don't mind. In the meantime, with regard to Mr Checket and Mrs Thurston . . . I suppose we had better let things ride. Dreadful expression – let things ride – don't you think?'

'I don't have much time for thinking about expressions. You won't mind if I don't see you out.' Veronica opened the file and began to study it with great intensity. She enjoyed such battles and entered them with patriotic fervour, as though she were defending some private territory.

Alisdair said goodbye with quiet courtesy and some restraint. Did Mrs Fairhurst always read notes upside down? He chuckled as he walked down the corridor. A new assistant might have thought him a recent admission.

CHAPTER
10

'Come out, wherever you are.' The song by Geraldo and His Orchestra had been resurrected for evening listeners. Peggy observed that very few could have been as deeply affected by the singer's dulcet tones as her friend Henry.

She sat half in her sleeping bag, resting against the wall, and viewed Henry as he sat in his bed. The night before he had called out for help, in the midst of some terrible nightmare. Peggy had woken him. Henry had told her something of his dream, and she knew it bore the imprint of a past reality.

'I was drinking in this pub. It was two bus rides from my bedsitter – but it was a nice friendly place. Run by two ladies – in the Balls Pond Road. And, can you believe it – there was a saxophone player. But it was a lady. It had been a nice evening. Always was, there.

'I left feeling happy and settled. On my way to the bus stop, two young men asked me for a light. Of course, as you know, I don't smoke so I couldn't help them. Can't remember a lot after that – being pushed to the ground and being kicked in the back and then a kick in the stomach. Knocked all the wind out of my sails – then the back of my head banged on the pavement. This voice said, "This man's not drunk. He's been physically attacked. He's concussed." I suppose it must have been a doctor – and after that I knew I was in a police station somewhere. These two policemen asking me questions, where I'd been and who had I been talking to in the pub and something about overtures. Couldn't understand it – I'd only been talking to Jean – she was the landlady of the pub. It was terrible. I felt as though *I* had done something wrong and after that – I never felt like leaving my room again . . .'

Peggy had told him the dream was all over – past – but she feared for her friend. And now this lovely music seemed to have upset him. When Peggy was upset, her friend Miss Lamb had often talked her to sleep, hadn't she?

'There's something I miss here, Henry,' Peggy called out, demanding his attention.

'Oh, what's that, Peggy? What is it you miss?'

'I miss having a cat. Do you like cats, Henry?'

'Never known one. Places I've been weren't allowed to have one.'

'After I'd been with Miss Lamb for about a year we found a wild, mackerel-tabby kitten in our garden. Oh, the state of it. It hissed and spat whenever you tried to get near it. Winter was close so we had to entice it gradually into the house with bits of food. Its wild head-box wouldn't have allowed it into our kitchen – but its belly talked louder.'

'Oh, I know what it's like to be hungry,' said Henry. 'And cold. That's a bad thing, too.'

'Well, Henry,' Peggy said, 'you wouldn't leave a kitten out in the cold, would you?'

'No, I suppose not, Peggy. I suppose not.'

'This kitten finally settled with us – but it must have had a bad time before. The state of it. Fleas all over, one eye half closed with flu. She threw up on the floor after being fed – threw up a load of worms. So, outside and inside, she was in a terrible way. But Baa-Baa gave it so much loving that in a month it was a changed creature. "Transformed," she said, "transformed. But, Peggy, we must not change its nature. I do feel that missionaries have probably achieved more lasting harm than good."

'Course, I couldn't see what missionaries had got to do with us two taking in a cat. With her dead father being a vicar you would have thought Miss Lamb would have been better disposed towards them. But she had no feeling for the cloth.'

'Was it a man or woman, boy or girl?' Henry asked.

'What? Miss Lamb?'

'No, the cat.'

'Oh, very much a lady, Henry. Very much a lady. She became so clean, and dainty. Always cleaning herself, preening and purring. She'd complain with loud miaows if her shit-box wasn't up to par. We had to change it completely – even after one little piddle. What a madam that cat was.'

'What did you call her?'

'Beryl. Miss Lamb said she reminded her of a friend at boarding school. They played in the netball team together. "Beryl! Beryl!" Miss Lamb would call her. She was big for a she-cat. Miss Lamb's friend had been a big girl as well. Beautiful, by all accounts.'

Peggy looked towards Henry anticipating a view of half-closed eyes and open mouth, the no-man's world between sleep and wakefulness. His mouth was closed and his eyes were wide open. His expression was interested and expectant. Her story was not sending him to sleep – it was keeping him awake.

'Mr Worrell asked for me to say goodbye to you, Henry. We're losing our favourite boilerman. He's gone to another job. Says we're not to go down to the basement anymore or she'll find out.'

'He must have known we went down there, then?'

'Yes – nice man. I wondered why the tea bags lasted so long. He left because she wanted him to stay down there all the time, not to mix with us as much as he did.'

'Terrible, terrible spending most of your life without seeing daylight. There were ponies in the pits when I was a lad – born there, they were. And when at last they brought them into the daylight – you know what?'

'What, Henry?' Peggy asked.

'They were blind – at least, they couldn't see anyway. All that time in the dark – and then no light.' Henry was surprised when Peggy started to cry a little. Just a few tears because of a bit of disconnected information. 'You never told me about the cat, Peggy. You never let me know about Beryl?' He enquired through Peggy's distress.

'Where did I get to, Henry? Where was I?'

'You said she was a big girl. Big for a female cat.'

'Oh, yes, well she just grew and grew, didn't she? Miss Lamb said we might get another one to keep her company – but she didn't seem to take very much to other cats that she met in the garden. So, I said that we could let nature take its course and we would keep her kittens when they arrived. When she called we'd let her have them.'

'Call? Call? What would she call for, Peggy?' Henry was astonished. Was Peggy making it up?

'Sex, Sexual intercourse. She-cats ask for it. But only when they are ready. Not otherwise. They have to be ready. Not like tom cats – dirty buggers. Never think about anything but that. Put it before food some of them do. But she-cats call. Then they have it – and then it's over with for a time.'

'Love don't seem to come into it much – does it, Peggy?'

'Well, I don't know. Perhaps it does. Beryl was ... well ... Beryl never called. She never asked for it. Even after she had gone well past the age she never called out. Just looked after her patch and let nothing near her.'

Peggy yawned and stretched her arms above her head. Patted her hair. Smoothed out the creases in her sleeping bag. Examined her roughened, hard fingers affectionately. Preened a little – and continued:

'Miss Lamb took her to the vet. I went with her. We sat on the bus together. Me, Miss Lamb, and Beryl in the basket. Miss Lamb talked to Beryl for the whole of the journey and some people gave Baa-Baa funny looks. As if to say she'd gone round the twist. But she took no notice. Lamb was like that. She didn't care for the usual niceties.'

Peggy began to laugh. 'Oh, Henry,' she chuckled. 'Oh, Henry.' There were tears of mirth now. 'She did lay the law down in that vet's. "As you are a male," she said to the vet, "it seems only right that Mrs Thurston and I should be present when you examine Beryl." Well, the man did seem to be a bit taken aback but he agreed to us being there. Animal doctors seem to be more co-operative than people doctors sometimes, don't they?'

'What did the doctor say? What was wrong with her?'

'"There's nothing wrong with her," he said. "She won't have kittens, Miss Lamb. They would have arrived by now if they were going to arrive."

'"Is it her womb – or . . . ?" Miss Lamb always had to know everything.

'"No, no, no," he said. "It's nothing physical. There's nothing physically wrong with Beryl. And she seems to have a very sunny personality." He began to stroke her. And that Beryl knew he liked her. Began to purr like a traction engine she did.

'Miss Lamb persisted. "Then why? Why?"

'"Beryl." The man coughed a bit. "Ahem! Ahem! Beryl is what we refer to as a recalcitrant quean. She is not – and will not be interested in male cats."

'"You mean we have a lesbian cat?" I thought Miss Lamb sounded more than hopeful when she asked this.

'"No, not quite. She doesn't want intimate sexual relations at all. And that's about it. I won't charge you for this. Perhaps you might like to donate something to one of the charities as you go out."

'I suppose Miss Lamb had began to think Beryl was like her. When, in fact, she was more like me.'

'Ah, but you called, Peggy. You called,' Henry muttered.

'Only once or twice.'

'It's enough, Peggy. It's enough.'

'Have you answered a call, Henry? If we had a kitten what would we name it?'

'Sax,' Henry answered without recourse to rumination. 'Sax. We'd call it Sax.'

'Oh, that's a good name. It wouldn't matter if it was a boy or a girl, or neither, with a name like that, would it?'

'Did it mind being on its own?' Here, Henry gently corrected himself, more in deference to the memory of Miss Lamb that the cat. 'Er . . . I . . . I mean, did she mind being on her own?'

'Well, she might have done, but we weren't to know, as another cat found us a couple of days later. I think cats do find people. One morning around ten o'clock Miss Lamb called me out to the front of the house. "Can you hear anything, Peggy?" she asked me. I said I could hear any number of things – traffic, calypso music, somebody working on a roof four doors down . . . "No, listen, listen, Peggy." Then I could hear the finest and faintest of mews. It was near, and it was a cry for help. We looked everywhere. Down on our haunches, looking underneath all the cars, in the sewage grid, everywhere we looked. It was only at the point of giving up that I put my ear to the bonnet of a car. We opened it, and there it was, a black kitten. Somebody had plonked it in there – so that when the engine started . . . oh, there are some cruel buggers about.'

'What was Beryl like with the kitten?' Henry asked.

'Like a mother. Cleaned it, fussed about it. But she did give it a swipe when it tried to latch on to her tits. 'Course we called the new kitten Madge, that was after an aunt of Miss Lamb. We had to change it later.'

'Why was that?'

'Well, it was a tom cat. As it got older it seemed to have no respect at all for Beryl wanting her private parts to herself – so we had to have his balls cut off.'

'Oh, how sad,' Henry cried out. 'Did he recover?'

'Yes, within a couple of hours. We called him Arnold from then on – Miss Lamb said that he might have an identity crisis otherwise. After the operation – you couldn't separate the two of them. Like Night and Day they were.'

'Just like lovers,' Henry observed.

'I don't think that two people or creatures or – whatever – have the leasehold on love just because they've jigged and poked about with one another.'

'Sometimes, Peggy, you talk as though you were a very rude nun.'

Peggy yawned. 'Do I? I don't think I'd mind being called Sister Peggy – only by you, though. But let's get this right, Henry. I'll swear to honour you but I'm blowed if I'll obey anybody unless I want to . . . and . . .' Peggy noticed Henry's open mouth, the closed eyes.

She crawled over to his bedside and switched off the light. She checked that his coverlet would not fall from his bed. She saw to his nightly comfort. She hoped that his dreams would be good – and then crept back into her sleeping bag and settled down.

Their night of dreams held no more confusions, bewilderments, joys or fears than the past day had done. Henry and Peggy lived in dawn and twilight – it was either a sense of the break of day or the impending sense of darkness that was approaching. In this light, they were ready to greet whatever came along. A prisoner of war, a saxophone player, a vicar's daughter, a cat, an ogre . . . they all danced out of light and into shadow or out of shadow and into light.

CHAPTER
11

———————————

'I'm off to the country this weekend. I'm sure I wouldn't be able to manage without my bolt-hole.' Veronica Fairhurst referred to her second home as though she were some unfortunate rabbit fleeing from rampant hounds.

'Allow about three-quarters of a pound of sugar to every pound of fruit.' She weighed the fruit with exactitude, taking one apple off the scales and placing another one on, until the arrow almost hit the desired mark. Accuracy was finally achieved by a sprinkling of blackberries.

For the last three Christmasses of exchange and mart present-giving she had given her close working colleagues a small jar of jam. Each jar sweetly wrapped and tidily labelled. 'I'm so glad you like it, dear,' she had said to one of the hard working West Indian care assistants who had looked at the watery concoction with some puzzlement. 'It's straight from the countryside, the English countryside. All of it natural, nothing added, home and country grown. The giving is all the more fun if there has been thought in the making of it.'

Veronica watched the fruit boil until it became soft and then turned off the gas. She sat down and gave out a self-satisfied sigh. This had nothing to do with the joy of her labour or culinary creativity. Her pleasure was based in prudent economic strategy. At the most, each jar of jam had cost fifty-five pence to produce. Not a lot to allocate to each and every one of her underlings, to whom she always gave the jam as though she were conferring some great privilege – as if it were some life-affirming nectar she had gleaned from the hedgerows. She added the sugar, waited for the fruit to set before squirting lemon juice from a plastic lemon into the centre of the jellied mixture.

She enjoyed the notion of her workers talking in her absence. 'Mrs Fairhurst has gone to the country for the weekend. She often spends weekends in her country cottage.' This picture of rural enchantment and homely virtues pleased Veronica. Anyone sitting in her present kitchen would see, however, that the portrait was duplicitous.

Veronica knew a bargain when she saw one. And when the council houses came up for sale in the swampy coastal region of the south east coast – she bought one. It had been a difficult house for the council to sell as it adjoined one other and was some six miles away from the ugly sprawl and shops that made up the nearest town. The bus routes from the town had been privatised and the company had gone bankrupt. The two houses were now left in isolation. Unless the occupants had a car or were extremely fit, this isolation was dire rather than splendid.

Like much public housing, it seemed to have been placed in the worst possible spot in an eroded countryside. The front of the house looked out on to a dreary salt-marsh and mud-flats. On a clear day, a strip of sea was visible and, sometimes, beyond the estuary the sky was lit by flames generated by cooling gases belching from iron towers. At the bottom of her garden a commuters' railway clattered throughout the day. There were fields and a few hedges on the other side of the track. So, technically, the countryside did exist.

In the summer the fields blossomed with a crude acid-yellow colour that dazzled the eye. Veronica had at first glowed with pleasure. Few other people could look out on mustard fields. Then she discovered that the yellow plant was not mustard but something vegetable oils were made from called 'rape' which bludgeoned her sense of wonder. The information had destroyed her 'summers'. Winter became her favourite country season.

It did not strike her as odd or unusual that she should buy

quantities of windfall apples in London and transport them to her grotto to make jam. Her husband had made a tentative reference to this (all his references were tentative and he rarely accompanied his wife to their cottage). Veronica had snapped at him. 'Just the making of it there is important. Think of what happened to our convicts when they sent them to Australia. Consider their transformation.' Her husband who had a more thorough grasp of history than his wife knew that these people had been subjected to the most grisly and vile times but sought not to mention it. He disliked jam, anyway, and was more attracted to savouries.

Veronica slowly ran a cloth over the already gleaming formica work surface. The domestic gadgetry assembled on it gave her some satisfaction. She recalled her own message at that staff meeting, nearly three years ago now, when she had brought the matter up as though it were an after-thought rather than something she had planned.

'Then, yes, there is just one more thing. If you could just bear with me for only a minute or two. It's . . . a little delicate – it's to do with your kindness towards me. We all need to be valued . . . yes, even me. And your presents at Christmastide never fail to touch me. I treasure every one of them. But I feel that I must ask you to desist from giving me any.' There had been murmurs of regret from some of her more sycophantic workers. She had continued on the theme before their murmurs died on the air.

'Yet, I would not want to take away the joy of giving. After all, that is what Christmas is all about. Wasn't the nativity babe given to us all? But like the shepherds we should offer only what we can afford. I don't feel that pockets should be unnecessarily stretched on my account. Therefore, I suggest – and it is only a suggestion – that a collective gift would be more suitable, that is, if you choose to give. I don't think any of you should spare more than one pound fifty each towards such a collection. There! I've said it. It was painful but sometimes one must face these things and, as you must know, it is all of you that I am thinking of. The value I place on you all goes well beyond the material. It is the thought that counts.' Veronica had managed to move herself close to tears by the quality of her own performance.

She looked at the blender, the double toaster, the boiling-jug that saved electricity and prevented water wastage. No one could have given less than a pound and the gifts were utilitarian as well as aesthetic. Thank God, she did not have to receive any more talcum powder that felt like grit and smelled of cheap dance halls. She assembled the jam jars – her own private enterprise was not without profit but there was great pleasure drawn from its making and the giving of it elevated the giver. Profit could be a saintly matter if it were properly presented.

It was in this sweet frame of mind that she entered her back garden. Even in winter it looked tidy; the tubs and gnomes were happily placed in their environment of concrete slabs. As she had said to the elderly man who lived next door when she had watched him dig up the last of his potatoes: 'I suppose vegetables have their place but they are so messy in a small garden. I would feel guilty about growing them, myself.'

'Guilty?' he had said as he scraped the mud from his fork.

'With such a food surplus. Europe, you know. It seems more responsible to buy potatoes rather than grow them. Think of the work it provides for other people. I wouldn't want to be selfish in such matters.'

For the life of him, the old man had not been able to see how growing a few potatoes, carrots and a bit of cabbage harmed anyone. He had sniffed noisily and decided she was soft in the head and only grunted in response to any greeting from her since.

In the afternoon light the jars of jam glowed like pale lanterns. Their incandescence, the visible proof of her industry and benevolence, cheered her. In her lined note-pad lying on the kitchen table she had written 'Projects'. Under this heading there was little to indicate any future plans. There were six names. The first three were: Peggy Thurston, Henry Checket and Alisdair McClennon. Veronica firmly believed that people controlled events. If you could control certain people then events happened as you wished them to happen.

Veronica had spoken to Peggy before she had left work on Friday. As she was leaving she had noted her sitting alone in the lounge. Peggy Thurston had gazed at her with unseeing eyes as she approached. The wretched old woman had looked smaller for some reason. Perhaps it was Henry Checket's great woollen cardigan encircling her shoulders which gave her such a shrunken appearance. As Veronica had got nearer she could hear strange blowing and whistling noises coming from Peggy's mouth. On the small table at Peggy's elbow stood a glass tumbler half full of water which magnified Peggy's dentures. They rested serene and calm, such ferocious looking things when taken out of the mouth.

'How are we today, then, dear? Sitting on our own, are we?' Veronica bent towards Peggy so that her eyes came directly into Peggy's view as she spoke. Veronica got no response from the eyes which looked more watery than usual. 'Feeling a bit down in the dumps, are we? Boy friend gone and left us, has he?' Still no response. The whistling and sucking continued as a faster pace.

Veronica felt the rush of excitement that made her frame tingle when she encountered an emergency. Was the old girl about to have a seizure? A stroke would place her elsewhere ... 'Mrs Thurston! Mrs Thurston!' Veronica tapped Peggy's shoulder. 'Are you with me, dear?' Her appeal was resonant and loud.

There were coughs and splutters. Eyes watering, spittle dribbling down the corner of the mouth. Time to ring for an attendant. Time to take control of the situation. And then Peggy had moved a claw-like hand. She had cupped it under the chin and ... and ... had spat something into the palm of her hand.

Veronica stared at the huge pear drop in dismay. 'Ah, we all ...'

'Piss off. Can't suck a pear drop in peace, here. I was enjoying that. You tapping at me as though I were a tin tack made me choke on it.' Peggy took the sweet and dropped it into the glass where it clattered to a stop on her dentures. 'Silly cow,' she muttered.

'Do you know who you are talking to, Mrs Thurston.'

'I wish I didn't.' Peggy eyed Veronica's suitcase.

'Travelling, are you? Like a pear drop for the coach?'

————————————

Veronica drew a line through Peggy's name. This indicated a personal defeat. She ruminated on Henry Checket. He, too, seemed to have gained a new obduracy – a new strength?

'Leave this to me.' Veronica had put on some rubber gloves and taken the garment away from her ancillary. She had sent for Henry and barely had given him time to sit down before she started. Henry had felt alarmed at the sight of the pink gloves. Hope she's not going to examine me – push her finger up my bum and things like that, he had thought. 'And what are these, Mr Checket?' Veronica had held the soiled directoire knickers between finger and thumb at arm's length away from her body.

'What are they, Mr Checket?'

'Knickers.'

'They were found in your room, Mr Checket.' She placed the knickers inside a plastic bag and put the bag on her desk as though it were some piece of treasured evidence. She smiled.

'I wonder if you would like to explain.'

'No, I wouldn't,' said Henry.

'I'm afraid, I'm very much afraid that you will have to.'

'I'm not the only one here who has a little accident now and again. Drunk too much tea before I went to bed. Got caught short.'

'You mean ...' Veronica had been genuinely taken aback by his boldness. 'You mean that these belong to ... to ... you?'

'Yes, I find them very warm in the winter months. I used to have two pairs. They've lasted well.'

'But ... but ... these ... these are for women ... they are women's wear.'

'Bought them years ago. Army surplus. WAAF's wear. That's why they're khaki.'

'Mr Checket, I'm surprised at you. Whatever would people think if they knew.'

'Which people? What people? Who has ever wanted to see me with my trousers off? Sometimes . . . sometimes . . . I think that men have to be more like women and women have to be more like men.' As he spoke he had stood, dismissing himself from the office, and snatched the plastic bag from the desk. 'I'll wash them through, myself. Always have in the past. Any number of women around here wear trousers. These keep my thighs warm. Not itchy about the shins, like longjohns.' He had left without her permission. He had washed Peggy's knickers and returned them to her.

True love of this kind was often based in kindly lies. Even Veronica knew this. She drew a line through Henry's name.

Only Alisdair's name was left. If there was some way to prove that his judgement was at fault. If she could orchestrate some kind of event that could go dreadfully wrong . . . perhaps then . . . she could begin eroding his status. What with diseases and social errors, bachelors were rarely out of the papers these days. Mr McClennon could hardly be described as a family man. He was no beauty to look at, but then, nowadays if a man earned a good salary, he ought not to be incapable of finding a wife.

As Veronica closed her mental filing cabinet she made preparations for bed. She checked the door locks, the windows. Left the kitchen in perfect order before looking at the task list that she had set for her husband. In her absence he was to hoover the house throughout, scrub the front doorstep, complete all personal and household laundry, polish shoes, clean windows upstairs and downstairs, both inside and out, video three late-night films, iron all clothing and sheets. She had discovered even before their marriage that the more imperious and authoritarian she behaved the better he seemed to like it.

Veronica saw nothing odd in requesting him to have his bath in the water that she left behind. Purely on the grounds of economy. The tepid water he seemed to find exhilarating. Sometimes she would say, 'Come into my bed.' He would dutifully obey, murmuring. 'Anything you say, you're the captain of the ship.'

It was a harmonious, tidy and ordered marriage based on mutual trust and shared understanding. Veronica's husband worshipped her, served, honoured and obeyed her and, like the good wife she was – she saw to it that he did. Any lapses were dealt with most firmly.

CHAPTER

12

It was early afternoon and it looked as if there ought to be snow but there was none. A sky constipated with snow refrigerated the city. Under low-hanging grey clouds, a strange light more reminiscent of dawn shed its pallor on to the steps leading from the french windows to the lawn. It was bitterly cold.

This was an important day for Henry and Peggy. They were about to embark upon a journey. A journey outside. This was an event; they had been making preparations for the trip for the last two and a half hours.

'There.' Peggy checked to see that the top button of Henry's great overcoat was fastened. 'Can you breathe all right?' Henry lowered the bottom half of his woollen balaclava helmet. 'Yes,' he replied and Peggy saw the human breath on the cold air. 'I'll just fasten my pixie-hood then we'll be off. Got to walk careful. Don't want to slip. If we hit the ground we'd crack a bone. No give in the earth today.'

Some of the ancillary workers had wanted to prevent them from making this journey. A trip to the bottom of the garden in weather like this was full of potential hazard. They had appealed to Mrs Fairhurst to intervene. To forbid this trip.

Her reply had come as a surprise. 'We cannot take away such a freedom. For others, the case might be different but you know how recalcitrant Mrs Thurston and Mr Checket can be. They have, as you know, taken the limits of individuality too far on many past occasions. If we question it . . . then . . . we are inevitably

wrong . . . I am tired of being called an ogre because of them.
She had left the lounge nodding and smiling and did not turn
round to watch the travellers step out.

She was ignorant of the fact that she, herself, had sown the
seeds of motivation for this trip in her pre-Christmas peroration
of plans for the festive season. There was to be a carol service
followed by a Christmas party and a concert two days later. There
were murmurs of appreciation and pleasure . . . but Veronica had
raised her hand and asked for quiet.

'But . . . but . . . you all know as well as I do that the spirit
of Christmas is not solely about receiving. No, it is about giving
too. Like the poor shepherds, many of you might ask "What can
I give?"'

'True, true . . .' called out an elderly woman, spellbound by
Veronica's rhetoric.

'Thrift, thrift . . .' Veronica had spoken out the words in a stage
whisper.

As most of the inmates had little saved and what was saved was
spent on luxuries that most people regarded as necessities, there
was an air of incredulity surrounding the now silent company.
'You cannot take out of the kitty what is not there; how can I
save thirty pounds, I asked myself? The answer came to me as I
painted my own bathroom door. Christmas decorations this year
. . . will be made by you. Everyone will give in this way . . . and
there will be a mystery prize for the best decorated bedroom.
When I walk around the building I shall look for paper chains,
lanterns, Christmas bells . . .'

'If we don't make any decorations, we don't have any dinner.'
Henry had let his bit of paper chain fall to the ground. 'I can't
lick this gum on the back. Makes me feel sick.' Peggy's attempts
had been worse. She sucked at her finger as the blood oozed
from a small wound. Her hands were no longer steady enough
for scissors and did things of their own accord refusing to obey
her brain. 'We don't have to do this, Henry,' she had declared as
she flung the scissors to the floor.

This is why they stood on the steps leading to the long garden.

At the bottom of the garden, past the flowerbeds, past the goldfish pond, past the small gazebo with the rotting roof, just beyond the orchard there were holly bushes.

Arm in arm, they made their way tentatively down the steps. 'What if it has no berries?' Henry asked. As if this barrenness indicated that the foliage had no right to exist.

'Holly is holly, Henry. Whether it has berries or not is none of our bloody business.' Peggy stopped to look at the goldfish pond as she answered him.

The pond was frozen hard. It was difficult to believe that this centre of life and activity was now dormant and still. They both contemplated the surface which looked like a bathroom window. The shapes beneath were blurred and indistinct. Only the orange and white colouring of the fish gave away their presence.

'They must be dead,' said Henry. 'Frozen to death. It's a good job we don't have to save on heating. I'm sorry they've gone. I'll miss seeing them next year.' Henry liked having things to look forward to.

'They're not dead, Henry. Oh, no, I can vouch for that.' Peggy reassured him. 'They might look as though they are ... but they're not.' She urged him slowly forward and talked.

'During the war, I can't remember the year but it was during the war. We had one hell of a winter. Snow! You have never seen the like of it. It froze hard the first day only to be followed by more and more of it. Any shopping Miss Lamb and me did, we used a sledge. Miss Lamb made it out of an old pram. We had to queue at the shops for everything. Bread, milk, potatoes. That snow imprisoned us. One Saturday we waited for four hours in the line for a bit of fish. Only to be told when it was our turn that there was none left. I don't know why, it wasn't like me, but I started to cry. And outside the shop I screamed at Miss Lamb: "I wanted some fish, just a little bit." Well, she calmed me down and patted my hand. I said I was sorry. After all it wasn't her fault that they had sold out.'

'Sometimes you can only be angry with people you like,' Henry observed.

Peggy was now as much involved in remembered soliloquy as she was in conversation. 'When we got home Miss Lamb said, "We'll get fish in the morning, Peggy. We'll get up early and get fish." I just nodded, thinking she might have gone a bit funny with all the strain and stress of things. The next day, it was a Sunday, I was sure that she had gone off her rocker.'

'Oh, dear, Peggy. Were you frightened?'

'She woke me up – it was still dark. "Time to get up, dear," she said. "There's a pot of tea made. We can have some breakfast when we get back."

'"Get back?" I asked. "Where the hell are we going?"

'"To get some fish, dear. I mentioned it last night." She spoke as cool as a cucumber. "Put plenty of clothes on. Wrap up well."

'I thought it better to humour her as best as I could and somehow get her to the doctor later on. So, there we were, dressed for Siberia and it wasn't even six in the morning. "I'll get my purse," I said. "Oh, you won't be needing that, my dear," she said. Then she went out to the back-kitchen and came back with the coal hammer and an empty potato sack.'

'Ooh . . . ooo . . . h . . . Peggy,' Henry exclaimed.

'I was so frightened I was near to being sick. It came into my head that she was going to kill the fishmonger. Now, he wasn't a bad person. He even preached at the Primitive Methodist chapel.'

'Well, if he was bad or good she oughtn't to hit him with a hammer.' Henry shook his head.

'I thought I'd go with her as far as the shop – then, when she got to the door – I'd scream and shout out warnings. But I didn't have to because we went nowhere near the shop.'

Peggy's story was interrupted by a flock of goldfinches searching in the old orchard for food. Suddenly disturbed by Henry's and Peggy's presence they flew off in a green and yellow flurry of wings. Henry and Peggy counted themselves lucky at viewing this flight. They would keep the incident to themselves as nobody at Restmore would believe they'd seen a flock of canaries. They might put them in a mental place if they talked about what they had seen.

'Where did you go, then?' Henry asked as he watched the finches speed out of view.

'We went out of the side of the village where the pit was. Past the pit – we trudged and on into the lanes. Not a house in sight. We got to the hump-backed bridge and we stood on top of it and looked at the water underneath us. Frozen solid. The canal was frozen hard. There were coal barges just stuck there in it. Oh, it was so quiet . . . so quiet the noise of your feet treading the snow seemed incredibly loud. You know, the countryside has just as much noise as the city but it was as though all the sounds had been frozen. Only us two, me and Miss Lamb moved and it's terrible to hear only your own footsteps. Like belching or farting at the wrong time or in the wrong place.'

'Oh, I've never done that Peggy. At least, not on purpose.'

'And then somehow, we got down the side of the bridge and on to the tow path. Miss Lamb took the coal hammer out of the potato sack and then gave me the empty sack to carry. I was going to say something then but she put her finger to her lip and frowned and walked on two paces ahead of me. I didn't want to follow her. I mean, if she had gone barmy she might have cracked me on the head with the hammer, mightn't she? And if I turned back without her – just like that, she might wander around until she was frozen solid. What could I do? What would you have done, Henry?'

'Well, I don't know because I wasn't there. But I think I might have followed her.' Henry did not like dilemmas. 'That's just what I did,' said Peggy as though she were now embarking on this adventure once again and taking Henry along with her. 'I kept a couple of yards behind her. What with the snow and ice under our feet it was a bloody slow crawl. And all the time Miss Lamb's eyes fixed and staring at the iced-up canal. She stopped just when we got to this small mooring basin. I remember that there were reeds stiff as pokers sticking up through the ice. Then she got flat on her stomach and stretched herself half over the edge of the canal bank.'

'Oh, God, had she gone mad,' Henry whispered.

'She half turned and asked me to hang on to her legs. I shook my head. She frowned and then the look on her face, oh, it was fierce. "Do it. Do what I say, Peggy." So I did. I sat on the middle of her legs and held on to her hips. And then . . . and then . . . she raised the coal hammer above her head and brought it down with the most almighty crash on the ice. Crack, it went, and the noise of it went ringing around our heads. Again and again she brought it down on the ice. "Hold on, Peggy, hold on, Peggy. I've stunned the bugger," she called out. All out of breath she was but she bashed at the ice . . . broke it . . . and floating on the water was a big fish. It seemed half asleep. She passed the hammer back to me, and with both hands she grabbed the fish and flung it onto the bank. It began to flop about a bit but she gave it a crack on the head with the coal hammer and that was the end of it.'

'It seems a lot to go through for a bit of fish,' Henry said thoughtfully. 'But if you wanted it badly enough I suppose you'd do it.'

'It wasn't a bit of fish, Henry.' Peggy's tone was a little peevish. 'It was a bloody big fish. Perhaps three or four feet long. Its head was a bit like a duck's head. Its jaws looked more like a bill. It was a pike, Henry. A pike . . . and Miss Lamb told me that royalty eat it sometimes. She baked it that day. Served it whole she did . . . and you know what . . . she stuck an apple in its mouth when it was placed on the table.'

'What did it taste like, Peggy?'

'Fish, Henry. Fish! That's what I wanted and that's what I got.'

'There's still three sitting there. Look!' Henry pointed at the goldfinches flitting from one bare fruit tree to the next.

'Now we've frightened them away.' She spoke in a sad, matter of fact voice. 'I've never seen canaries outside before. I suppose they're scrabbling for food. It's a bad thing to scrabble for food.'

'Oh, I know, I know.' Henry spoke from the harshest of personal experiences. 'But don't feel badly about the birds, Peggy. It's not us who frightened them away. It's that.' He pointed to the magpie which chattered coarsely as it flew to the ground. 'Salute it, Peggy! Salute it. Or we'll have sorrow.' Henry stood to attention and saluted the bird. Peggy did likewise, not from fear or superstition but . . . well . . . if it meant something to Henry.

From the french windows, Alisdair McClennon looked out at the view. He was perplexed by Henry and Peggy's actions. Were they involved in some private, elderly, military tattoo? Is that what senility was? A search for a deeper privacy? He saw their arms drop. The saluting over, Henry was pointing once more.

'Oh, there's another one. Joined its mate. There's two of them. There's two.'

'Eh! What's going on, Henry?'

'There's two magpies, Peggy. Two. Two for joy. Two for joy,' he cried.

Peggy was glad that Henry was happy. She took his arm and they began their slow journey once more. 'Two's a pair. Takes two to tango. Two for company.' Peggy had never felt coupled before and gripped Henry's arm more tightly in order to reassure herself she was not dreaming.

Their slow but eventful journey took them past the neglected and barren orchard to the perimeter of their universe, a thick hedgerow of holly and rhododendron which hid the road from view. Beyond the dark-green leaves was a world from which they had now retreated. They stood for a short time listening to a wailing police car shriek past. Even in their present setting the noise carried transient distress.

Peggy broke this small self-indulgence by snapping off some large sprays of holly from one of the bushes. She called over her shoulder. 'Come on, Henry, we don't want to hang about. We don't want a cold for Christmas.'

'There's no berries on it, Peggy. You can't have holly without berries.' In spite of himself Henry joined her activity.

'You can have holly without berries, Henry, because this is holly and it hasn't got any. The birds ate them. You wouldn't want the birds to starve, would you?'

'Oh, no, I wouldn't want that.'

'Well, that's that, then. Just a few more sprays and we'll have enough.'

Peggy's matter of fact outlook was somehow always tinged with a little hope. This particular brand of idealism offered him enthusiasms without disappointments.

The snow began to fall before they had completed half their return journey. It was a fine, powdery variety of snow, small particles rather than great flakes. It produced an effect of making the physical and human geography of the scene look as though it had been showered with talcum powder.

On a more pressing and practical level its presence offered little comfort to Peggy or Henry. It hindered their vision as the particles seemed to attack their eyes. 'We'll shelter in here for a bit.' Peggy drew Henry into the crumbling gazebo. Part of the roof was still intact and a meagre cover was better than none at all.

There was a vague smell of ... could it be scent? Alisdair McClennon sniffed. Something half way between lavender and disinfectant? He glanced sideways to find Veronica Fairhurst had joined him. Such was the extent of his preoccupation that he had not heard her approach. The expression on his face drew her response.

'I do hope I haven't startled you, Mr McClennon. I didn't mean to creep up on you. Now, I've broken your reverie. I wish that I had more time to dream. And what can we do for you today?'

'I'm not here in an official capacity, Mrs Fairhurst. This is not a working day . . . just visiting friends.'

'Ah, Mr Checket and Mrs Thurston . . . they are out there somewhere. There was nothing that I could do to restrain them. An odd day for touring the garden, don't you think?'

'They are sheltering in the gazebo, or what's left of it.'

'This time next year, there'll be nothing left of it. The council have sold off the land from that point to where the garden meets the road. It's gone to a company who are to build a number of small town houses. So our neighbours will be a nice class of people. I suppose we should feel grateful for that. An orchard almost in the centre of the city is a luxury the nation simply cannot afford. I take rather a patriotic outlook about such things.'

'Patriotism is sometimes strangely rewarded. In their time . . . in their time . . . both Mr Checket and Mrs Thurston have been patriots and some might feel that their efforts in the past might have entitled them to the use of a large garden in their declining years.' Alisdair paused, then added: 'I've come to let Mr Checket and Mrs Thurston know their wedding arrangements. Arrangements is hardly the right word, as I only have to give them a time, date and place.'

'I think you might have forgotten one detail, Mr McClennon – as a bachelor we can forgive you that. Witnesses! In all truth, I don't think I can find anyone here who could witness such a union and believe that they were acting in good faith. It's just a question of conscience. I'm sure you understand.'

'Yes, I do,' Alisdair murmured. 'There are three witnesses.'

'I cannot believe that anyone who has known either of them could possibl. . .'

'I am one witness. Mrs Mumbry is another, and Mr Worrell makes it three. The marriage will have witnesses, Mrs Fairhurst.'

'Mrs Mumbry! Not the one who was Mrs Thurston's social worker. And that man who used to see to our boilers. Well, I wonder what on earth the three of you have in common?' Veronica spoke lightly.

'Our common thought is for the future happiness of the pair. You wouldn't want to question that?' Alisdair found it hard to keep a trace of exasperation from entering his usual level tones.

'No, no, no, Mr McClennon. Now while I've got you here I wonder if I might go through our Christmas arrangements with you. I know how busy you are – but if you could get yourself along to one of our little events . . . er . . . I'd be most grateful.'

Veronica extolled the coming events. Who would be attending, times, dates . . . her voice rising and falling as her enthusiasms mounted. Alisdair looked out on the garden as he listened. The snow continued in its light descent.

'There's an animal there.' Henry gripped Peggy's arm and pointed to the opposite corner of the gazebo. Peggy edged forward to scrutinise the still form. She bent low over it, straightened up and sighed deeply.

'It's a cat, a tabby cat, a mackerel-tabby cat. Come and see, Henry. He's gone, poor thing. Dead. He's begun to stiffen already.' Henry looked closely at the cat. He was not morbidly curious, but there was something about it . . . something . . . which reminded him of . . . He bent down and stared at the glazed eyes and half-open jaws. From the side of the mouth a trail of yellowish saliva still trickled slowly down. 'Ah . . . ah . . . ah . . .' Henry gasped as he was transported back in time. It was not a love object that sharpened his vision of the past.

The hut was surrounded by jungle. From the open entrance the view was of palm and bamboo. The sick and ill had been left there when the allied armies commenced their liberation. Were there twelve or fifteen men? No water, no food. How many days had they been lying here? Groans, stench, excrement and flies. Flies everywhere, nowhere private. But Henry could still crawl and managed to help the other men drag their dead compatriots out of the hut. No, oh, no, he would not drag Charlie out. No, he was not dead. 'Look, look, you silly bugger . . .' The young soldier had seized Henry by the hair and pulled his face to within a few inches of Charlie's mouth. The yellow bile and spittle oozed from the lips and trickled down his chin on to his neck and chest.

Henry helped drag the body to the edge of the bamboo thicket. The other two men crawled back to the hut. Henry had sat there making a strange wailing noise like some animal that was caught in a snare. This stopped as he began to snap off the bamboo leaves and throw them over Charlie's body. He continued with this frenzied activity until he . . . until he went blank.

'Ah, ah, ah,' Henry cried out. 'Peggy, Peggy, Charlie's dead. He was always dead. I've been searching for him all these years and he was dead before I began to look for him.' Henry sobbed noisily. His head hung forward on his chest.

'Not time wasted. It wasn't time wasted, Henry.' Peggy's unexpected and unsentimental response caused Henry to jerk his head up from his chest.

'Eh? What's that you say, Peggy?' he asked.

'Well, if you hadn't been searching for Charlie you might just as well have been searching for another man. The man inside your head couldn't have been Charlie, but whoever he was, he wasn't too bad or your mind wouldn't have stayed with him all these years, would it. We can't leave that cat there, can we, Henry?'

'No, that wouldn't be right,' agreed Henry.

'Put it inside your overcoat and we'll give it somebody indoors to bury for us. Snow or no snow we'll have to make our way back. Don't want to be here when it gets dark, do we?'

'No, Peggy, we don't.' Henry obeyed her and followed on behind as she stepped out into the snow.

———————

'We have quite an adventuresome programme for our concert, ah, and I quite forgot to mention our Fancy Dress Evening. We are starting our festive season with a Fancy Dress Evening. The suggestion came from Mr Nigel Gobling, headmaster of one of our local primary schools. He is bringing over some children and they will join some of our residents. He is going to think up a special theme so that young and old can unite as well as compete. Can we tempt you to come along as something other than yourself, Mr McClennon?' Veronica tried her best to sound coy. 'I'm afraid my imagination is limited,' Alisdair lied happily. 'I'm sure that the concert will be to my liking. I'll attend that.' He broke off to point in the direction of the lawn. Peggy trudged towards them. The fine snow had settled on the woollen fabric of her coat and pixie-hood so that a complete white figure, timeless and ghostlike, approached them.

'What on earth does she look like?' Veronica half exclaimed, half questioned. They watched Peggy stop walking. She stood quite still for a few seconds. And then turned slowly to beckon Henry to her side.

'Subject matter for your competition. Lot's Wife. There she is turning.' Alisdair spoke more to himself than to Veronica.

'Oh, I do hope we won't have any characters as bad as that, Mr McClennon.'

'I'm not a fundamentalist, Mrs Fairhurst – I've always thought that Lot's wife was rather harshly and unfairly treated. It might not have been a morbid or vicarious pleasure that caused her to turn.'

'Surely, you would not wish to condone the behaviour of harlots and sodomites and the like?' Concern and elation seemed to be mixed in Veronica's questioning.

'It is conceivable that Lot's wife might have turned to look round for compassionate reasons. As for behaviour, past behaviour . . .' Here Alisdair gazed directly into Veronica's eyes. 'As for past behaviour and how it is judged, Mrs Fairhurst, I would remind you that Christ himself chose a common prostitute as one of his handmaidens.'

Peggy and Henry had reached the bottom of the steps leading up to the french windows. 'I haven't time to philosophise, Mr McClennon. I'd like to . . . but this job of mine has more pressing details that need to be attended to. I'll see you at the concert . . . perhaps?'

'Definitely!' Alisdair called after her retreating form. With the Bible still on his mind he muttered, 'Fucking philistine.'

'What's that you say, Mr Mac?' Peggy gasped a little. 'Did I hear you say a bad word?'

'Oh, no, you couldn't have. Mr Mac wouldn't say a bad word.' Henry was often generous in this way. Alisdair ignored Peggy's question.

'I just popped along to give you the date. The date of your wedding. It's Thursday, the eighth of January, at eleven-thirty a.m. The registry office – as you both requested. Mrs Mumbry, Mr Worrell and myself are to act as witnesses. We will provide transportation, of course. Alisdair found himself using the formal language of his occupation. He often retreated into this formality in order to hide the caring side of his nature. It was a mystery, even to him, why this was so.

'How kind you are to us, Mr Mac.' Peggy responded politely.

'It's my job, Mrs Thurston, just my job.' Alisdair found Peggy's gratitude embarrassing.

'Oh, no, it's not. You could do your job without being kind. Couldn't he, Henry? He's got a kind face, hasn't he, Henry?' These questions only increased Alisdair's discomfort.

'Well, I just thought that I'd let you know. Keep you informed. If there is anything else that you want ... er ... I'm sure you will let me know.' Alisdair made as if to leave before he finished talking. Peggy restrained his quick departure by holding a holly branch before him.

'Oh, there's just one thing. I'm sure you won't mind, Mr Mac. Henry, give it him now.'

Alisdair felt himself blush and was quite glad that his frequent drinking sessions had given his face a permanent alcoholic glow which camouflaged such betrayals of feeling. The idea that this elderly couple should wish to give him a present for merely doing what he was paid to do irked him. He was about to go into a small diatribe on serving the community but remained silent as he watched Henry place his holly boughs on the floor. Alisdair's curiosity was beginning to overcome his professional scruples.

Henry had great trouble in unbuttoning the top of his overcoat. His fingers were cold and the coat seemed to be very tightly pulled across his chest. 'There!' Henry gasped with relief as the waistline button finally let go of its mooring. He began to heave and tug at something somewhere close to his heart. Something bulky.

'I wonder if you would mind giving it a decent burial, Mr Mac.' Peggy referred to the dead tabby cat which Henry held out to Alisdair. 'We found him out there in the summerhouse. Poor old tom cat. He was probably making his last search when the cold caught up on him. It's over for him now. No more voyaging. No more chasing. It comes to us all.'

Henry placed the cat in Alisdair's hands. He then bent and picked up his holly, and he and Peggy made their way slowly into the house leaving Alisdair outside on the steps. Alisdair did not follow them but closed the door behind their retreating forms. He hurried down the steps into the garden. He turned left at the ornamental pond and followed the pathway which led him to the dustbins. He looked about him to check if his actions were being observed. He took old newspapers from the top of one bin and wrapped the creature in them before dumping it into one that was half empty.

Later, while he was washing his hands inside the house Alisdair was surprised that he did not feel relieved or unburdened after ridding himself of the sickening, nauseous creature. Peggy's words sounded in his head. 'It comes to us all.' He continued to let the warm water from the tap splash over his hands. Peggy and Henry had not grieved greatly over the cat. They had not asked him to grieve over it. He supposed he could and should have buried it at least on health grounds. And by his own high standards his action had been morally at fault.

He had been asked to honour the dead. A decent burial . . . a simple request from an aged woman who could share Antigone's sentiments about . . . not a relative . . . but a beast.

CHAPTER
13

ENTERTAINMENT FOR OLD FOLK

Mr Nigel Gobling, the enterprising young headteacher
of St Zeta's Primary School has planned to celebrate
the real spirit of Christmas. Next week he and eight of his
pupils are to join the residents of Restmore Old People's
Home for a special Fancy Dress Party.

'We should not forget our elderly at this time of family
re-unions,' Mr Gobling said. 'The spirit of Christ is
epitomised by this project for the young and the old to join
together. I hope we can breathe fresh air and life into
lonely, old people who may think that they are forgotten.'

Mr Gobling, headteacher of Zeta's for the last two
years, previously held the post of deputy-headteacher at
Samaritan Way Junior Mixed School. He received his
B. Ed (Hons) in 1980 and is married and has two children
aged three and five. The theme of the Fancy Dress Party
is appropriately Ancient and Modern.

Veronica held the local newspaper in her fingertips as though
it was contagious. She scrutinised the photograph of this Mr
Gobling which took up as much space as the article itself.
Enterprising! Veronica had never seen anyone to whom such a
description applied less.

A wide-browed man with short hair plastered down to reveal

a widow's peak gazed out from the page. He stared from behind large, dark-rimmed spectacles. Underneath an aquiline nose thin lips appeared to be on the verge of a tightly controlled smile. His tie was of the striped variety that indicated that he belonged to something – there were any number of clubs for advancement.

Veronica correctly conjectured that Mr Gobling had himself engineered this press release. He probably had an application for a bigger school in the pipeline. Or perhaps he was in the running for some position higher up the scale? She flung the newspaper into her waste bin. Unpaid self promotion, that's all it was. Using Restmore for his own advantage.

It was only four-thirty in the afternoon and this Mr Gobling's self-aggrandisement had compounded a number of disappoint-ments and irritations earlier in the day. Mrs Valerie Smith-Powell, the leader of the council had arrived at eleven-thirty to judge the room decorations and announced that a prize of five pounds was to be given to the one she considered the best.

'I have chosen this room because it illustrates the naturalness of Christmas. It gives us an idea of the passing of time – and some idea of a time when people had to do things by their own initiative. And they were none the worse for that. This holly is so reminiscent of the British character. If one tries to pillage it one is left with bloodied hands. I have no difficulty in announcing Mr Checket's room as the winner.'

Veronica had been flabbergasted by Mrs Smith-Powell's speech. It had got worse when Peggy had shuffled forward with Henry. She had taken the cheque, smiled graciously at Mrs Smith-Powell, thanked Veronica herself for organising the competition and told Mrs Smith-Powell of her forthcoming mar-riage. She had held up the cheque and said, 'It takes a woman to manage the pennies, doesn't it?' Mrs Smith-Powell had led the applause.

As if all this wasn't enough, the residents appeared to have gone on a subdued kind of strike over their midday meal. It was Veronica herself who had suggested to the cook that a little well-judged austerity with regard to meals preceding Christmas lunch might well enhance the reception of the lunch when it finally came, as well as avoiding over-spending the budget. She was not the first to practise this elegant form of economy.

The residents had not refused the spam fritters, the instant mash potato, nor the dyed, vivid green peas. They had just moved the food around a bit on their plates and left it. For the very old, a meal such as this could be left aside without any feelings of guilt. If someone else were starving somewhere else, then give it to them. A wretched meal like a wretched day could be easily forgotten when you forgot about so many other things.

Veronica smiled and thanked God for her inspiration; the spam fritters could be offered to Mr Gobling and his band of junior revellers. Cut into strips and decorated with a few of the peas they would be a most attractive looking little nibble. And she had read somewhere that children should be encouraged to eat savouries. The biscuits and cakes could be held back for the sole consumption of her own residents. The Fancy Dress Party was not to begin until seven p.m. so there was plenty of time to arrange things with the catering staff.

———————

Peggy pressed the loose end of the plaster firmly down on Henry's left buttock. 'There! There! I don't want you to have a sore bum.' A visitor entering the room might have wondered, and even re-thought his ideas about the sexual activities of the elderly. But first glances are often misleading.

Henry's trousers and underpants hung about the calves of his legs. He was bent forward, supporting himself with his hands on the bed. Peggy knelt behind him. His buttocks loomed white and large like two half-moons less than six inches from her face.

She surveyed her nursing which had decorated Henry's behind with three sticking plasters. 'You can pull them up now.' Peggy's voice contained a trace of satisfaction. As Henry struggled to adjust his dress she added: 'Oh, God, Henry, when you called out like that I thought you were having a heart attack. It was my fault leaving that holly on the chair. It must be a wicked plant to sit on.'

Henry answered her that it was and wondered why they couldn't change to a more tender plant for Christmas, something like privet or laurel. He was pleased to see Peggy opening the large box of chocolates that had accompanied their prize. They had decided not to share the chocolates or the money, as both of them felt that they had earned them. The chocolates could be written off as an *ex gratia* award, a compensatory gift for Henry's present injuries, and as neither of them had eaten any lunch, they had decided a private feast was sometimes more enjoyable than a collective one.

The opened box of chocolates was placed between them as they sat on either side of the bed. Peggy had discovered a pencil somewhere in the recesses of her clothing and began to prod each chocolate with its sharpened end. The soft centres were revealed this way without the flavour being known beforehand. The hard ones could be sucked at leisure at a later time.

There was scant time for conversation. Their hands alternated with cormorant-like skill. As one chocolate dissolved it was quickly replaced by another. 'What bliss,' Peggy thought as the coffee cream whirled about her gums. She felt very happy indeed. 'What was it that Miss Lamb had said about the very happy day they had spent in Brighton? Ecstatic! That was the word.' In between salivating and swallowing Peggy said, 'Can we go to Brighton for our day's honeymoon trip, Henry. Mac said he'd take us out for the day.'

'I don't know whether I've been there or not, Peggy.'

'Don't speak when you're eating chocolate, Henry.' Peggy wiped some brown dribble from Henry's chin as she chided him gently.

Peggy mused aloud before plopping another chocolate into her mouth. 'You couldn't forget Brighton if you'd been there.' Miss

Lamb had often given her chocolates. She thought of her now: 'We'll visit my aunt tomorrow, Peggy. The only living relative I am really fond of. She lives alone in Brighton. The sea air will do us both good and I think you'll like my aunt and her house.'

Peggy had not been enthusiastic. Miss Lamb's social background held fears for Peggy that she could not put into words. For some reason, Peggy was unable to accept patronage. She could sniff it a mile off, no matter how gracious or subtle the delivery. What kind of woman would this aunt be? Living all by herself in a house all to herself at the seaside.

That taxi journey from the station which had taken them down to the seafront. Miss Lamb asked the driver to progress slowly along the sea road. As they passed the splendid white-painted Regency houses and wonderful terraced crescents Peggy's misgivings increased. Thank God she put on her best frock and her court shoes. Perhaps if she didn't speak when she got there, perhaps if she could pretend that she were deaf and dumb she might not let Miss Lamb down.

She glanced nervously at her friend who made no concessions towards outward appearance. If Peggy didn't know her she would have mistaken her for one of those lady gardeners who wore green jerseys, brown slacks, and wellingtons – even in the warm weather. The taxi moved slowly on. The hotels, the crescents, the large balconied white houses seemed to come to an end. The cab turned inland away from the sea.

Immediately behind the grand coastal facade the houses began to get smaller. Some of them couldn't possibly have boasted a garden. There was the same type of net curtain at the windows that spelt out 'poor but clean' elsewhere. The cab turned into a narrow side road with mean-looking little terraced houses on either side. Looming over them, casting a deep shadow on the already gloomy looking street was an olive-green gasometer.

'I have forgotten the number but if you drive slowly, I'm sure that I will be able to recognise it from . . . ah . . . stop . . . stop . . . stop just here. This is sure to be the one. Yes, this must be the house.' Miss Lamb pointed to a house whose paintwork had a faded and flaking appearance. The window panes appeared to be spattered with mud. This puzzled Peggy as there had been no rain for days. As they approached the doorway her puzzlement increased as she saw two birds – not hens – flutter and perch on the window sill inside the house. One of the birds excreted leaving a testament to its presence to run down the window pane.

Peggy chuckled and shoved another chocolate into her mouth. 'What a sight that Aunt Angela was . . . What a sight! Must have been older than I am now,' she thought. 'At least I don't have bits of straw in my hair.' Miss Lamb's aged relative looked as though she had spent a few nights in a barn. And that was what the inside of the house resembled – a barn.

Angela greeted them warmly but Peggy had sniffed before she returned a verbal greeting. It was an animal smell, fecund, strong. Not unlike a chicken run or a stable – or a mixture of both. As they walked down the hallway into the back kitchen a duck squawked and followed them from its resting place in the tiny front lounge.

Miss Lamb and her aunt seated themselves on what looked like a pew that had been torn from some church. Peggy was directed to the only armchair but hovered about it because yet another duck was happily settled on its cushion. Angela motioned and muttered something. The duck rose, left the chair and waddled towards her. Peggy almost sat down . . . 'Wait!' Angela restrained her and retrieved something from the cushion. 'There! You can have that for your tea.' Peggy stared at the egg resting in Angela's palm – such a pale-green colour.

Lost in reverie, Peggy searched for another chocolate. The needs of the present focused her eyes on the box. It was empty. She looked up and gazed at Henry. His skin seemed to have changed colour.

'Do you like duck eggs, Henry?' she asked.

His eyes bulged. He retched. Peggy held the empty chocolate box to his chest as he vomited. Peggy shook her head. 'You shouldn't be greedy, Henry. Look what it does for you. Now, drink a glass of water and you'll be all right.' Henry spoke to her in a peevish tone. After all, she'd eaten as many chocolates as him and not been sick. 'It was the duck egg that did it,' he defended himself quietly. His nausea now left him. He rejoined Peggy and sat on the bed.

'Sorry about that, Henry,' Peggy apologised matter-of-factly. 'I can't say that I enjoyed it that much myself.' She smacked her lips and clicked her tongue in remembrance. 'Strong flavoured it was – I ate a lot of bread with it and it still tasted like cod-liver oil and that stuff we spooned down our gullets during the war. But what a day it was! We laughed and talked and that Aunt Angela swore like something I'd never heard before, and believe me, I've been around some places in my time. I wondered what her neighbours might think about the way she lived and how she was and all – the birds and things . . .'

'Oh, Peggy, they couldn't have liked it. It wasn't really the place to have a farmyard, was it. I mean . . .'

Peggy cut in on Henry carried away with enthusiasm for the past. 'Her neighbours? They didn't care a bugger. We went out into the tiny back garden. The afternoon was warm and there we sat on the bench with birds fluttering about us. Her neighbours called out greetings. They waved to us. There were four of them. Four men. Angela called them "the boys". They did dress a bit young for their age, and two of them wore earrings. One looked like a bricklayer and the other was a bit overweight and wore a tee shirt with something written all over it.' Peggy shook her head. 'No, they weren't boys – but you couldn't have guessed their age. It would have been easier to win a raffle than do that.'

'We hadn't been sitting there for more than twenty minutes before out they came again. One had a tray with cakes on it. And another one carried a large glass jug of red-coloured drink with ice cubes and fruit floating in it. There was even a great big yellow parasol, and the one with the tee shirt brought out a bowl of fruit.

'Were they having a party?' Henry's interest seemed to have quickened.

'Oh, no, Henry. They weren't having a party, they were giving us one. It's true, it's as true as I'm sitting here. Angela introduced us all. Can't remember their names now. Then they just passed everything over to us. We were all chaffing and laughing over the fence.' Peggy paused. 'You know, I never knew Miss Lamb ever to talk with men that much – not ever. But with that lot she was gabbing ten to the dozen. After she'd drunk a couple of glasses of this red drink with fruit in it she said it was nice that Angela had some of their brothers as neighbours.'

'Brothers?'

'Yes, I was a bit taken aback – but she just said that in some ways they were soul-mates. I couldn't think she meant it in a religious way – because of her father being a vicar he'd knocked all that out of her in one way or another.'

'They sound very interesting, Peggy.' Henry wanted to know more.

'Miss Lamb said they were exotic or ecstatic – or something like that. I think ... I think ... at a different time ... in a different place ... I think you might have been happy with them, Henry.'

'I'm happy enough now,' said Henry, and then added dolefully, 'Oh, Lord, Peggy, we've got this Fancy Dress tonight. And we haven't thought of what to wear.'

'We can go as Adam and Eve. Wear bugger all. Go naked into the world.' Peggy spoke sharply.

'Oh, no, no, I couldn't do that, Peggy. No, I couldn't do that. No, never.' He shook his head to give his observation extra emphasis.

'If you don't mind me saying so, Henry, that's one of your problems.'

'Problems! You've never gone naked have you, Peggy?'

Peggy laughed aloud. 'Me? Me? I've gone naked all my life, darling.'

'Nobody ever called me darling before.' Henry was touched.

'I never ...' Peggy stopped. She had only used the word with Miss Lamb. She had only ever used it devotionally. She shrugged her shoulders at this small, tragic thought. 'I'll think of something for us to wear. We won't go naked, Henry.'

'There's a gasometer in Accrington as well,' said Henry.

Peggy muttered, 'Oh, yes.' One minute you were in Brighton, the next you were naked, and then you were in Accrington. You never knew whether you were on your arse or your elbow with Henry at times. Now was that Fancy Dress thing tonight? Or tomorrow? Or had they already taken part in it? Anyway, they'd dress up. They could always put on a dressing gown if the time was wrong. Time – no need for clocks now – it went backwards and forwards – backwards and forwards.

CHAPTER

14

————————

Veronica moved from behind her desk and sank into one of the empty visitors' chairs. She ignored the slight draught from the nearby window and let her arms flop to her side. She acted as though she had been winded by some tremendous blow in the stomach. Yet, though there was no pain and no gasping for breath, she just sat, legs splayed and arms akimbo. Was it possible for a telephone conversation (and a short one at that) to create this state of being? The call itself had been short.

'Hello, Mrs Fairhurst? Yes, this is Alisdair McClennon speaking. I came across a report in the local paper.'

'Yes. That headmaster. I'm rather dismayed by it,' Veronica had replied in a controlled, mournful tone.

'Dismayed! You ought to be bloody furious.' This retort she had taken as an enormous compliment. Alisdair had never made her feel valued before, not in any way.

'But I am. I am furious, Mr McClennon.'

'Used! Used! That's how you must feel. That patronising swine. What a bloody joke. It's his own promotion he's interested in. Does he think that you don't provide a very good home for your residents? Well, he's wrong, you do . . .' Veronica was stunned by his vehemence. Her grievance towards the 'enterprising' young headteacher – Mr Nigel Gobling – began to fade into the background. 'I'll come to the Fancy Dress tonight. I'll cancel my other meeting.'

'That is good of you. I'll be most grateful for your support. I . . .

I . . . hadn't thought that you thought so much . . .' Veronica's voice faded as Alisdair's cut in.

'I'll arrive half an hour or so before it all starts. Give us a few minutes to talk.' The phone had clicked, she had replaced the receiver and now she sat marooned in thought.

Veronica had never felt so truly valued and appreciated and, apart from the balm offered in the words, Alisdair's manner had affected her heart. This was most unusual. Somehow she managed to stand up and walk over to the cabinet where she kept the special dry sherry. The thimble-like glasses were more suitable for an eye-bath than for drinking. She took a long hard swig from the bottle like a hero in a Western film and felt distinctly better. Her heartbeat was just as fluttery but her knees, arms, and other joints appeared to have joined her body again. In a most unprofessional way – what Mr McClennon had done was to enter her own personal suffering. This was one of the few times that she could not only feel but *be* properly indignant. But was it this indignation that made her feel . . . yes, excited? No, it couldn't be that.

For his part, Alisdair looked about the café where he sat eating a dish piled with jam roll and custard. From time to time he licked the custard away from his untidy moustache, the contours of which had crept over his top lip and curled into his mouth. He could feel the hairs on his tongue when he licked his teeth. The exercise gave an added pleasure to the meal and in his present surroundings nobody would be too concerned with table manners.

Looking around at the other customers, Alisdair almost felt as though he was at work. But, everyone was well over sixty years of age – or at least looked it, and seemed to ponder and pick for hours over a buttered bun and a cup of tea. The four women present sat at separate tables entirely alone. It was very quiet. At lunchtimes the place was busy with working men who ate noisily and spoke in a ribald fashion to each other. At such times Alisdair enjoyed the place.

Now, it was five p.m. the betting shops had closed and this

present group of men had left one warm place for another. In a betting shop, it was warm; you could watch the TV. It was free – and you could talk if you wanted to. Alisdair muttered to himself: 'If the libraries and betting shops closed through the winter, a fifth of the population might die of hypothermia.' He glanced again at the offending newspaper report with the photo of Mr Gobling – took another mouthful of jam roll and decided that he would opt for early retirement in the approaching New Year.

It was too much like a workplace for him to linger over his tea. There could be no vicarious pleasure from admiring the looks of dark-haired and moustached men whose fathers had been of Greek or Turkish origin. It was a small secret pleasure as Alisdair had only ever looked. Nothing more – he sighed as he rose from his chair. He had not needed a vivid sexual imagination to maintain his celibacy. The reality had often been about him, and his regret was that at points in time when he might have indulged it, he had not. On so many occasions he had remained silent when he should have spoken out. A whisper, even, might have been better than . . .

As he walked along the pavement towards his car an arm stretched out from the doorway of a derelict shop. He almost paused to see what this reaching out was about. But thought better of it. If you paused in the city for all that was drawing you, you might well be pulled under. Community care – what a bloody joke. He laughed bitterly and was about to quicken his step when he heard the voice.

The Scottish accent he could place to within a few miles of where he had been born. The remnants of his own family meant very little to him. A cousin or so would send a card at Christmas but his memory of childhood and family life did not leave him nostalgic. A rigid, punitive Catholic upbringing had not suited him – and when at twenty-three he was told by his father that it was unnatural not to be married, he had decided not to visit home again. He had wanted to say: 'But it would be a delinquent thing for me to *be* married,' but had remained quiet and smiled in a sad, passive kind of way. With these thoughts in his head, he had retraced his steps and made his way back to the Scottish tones that called to him from the doorway. Roots could not be so easily left behind and the accent beckoned him.

He saw, sitting in the midst of great piles of newspapers and cardboard boxes, a man of his own age. Perhaps he might have been ten years younger. Social dereliction and neglect affected people in the same way as it did buildings. Alisdair expected the smell of alcohol or spirit to waft in his nostrils. He was surprised to find that this was not the case. He looked about the man and saw no empty bottles. He waited for the man to speak . . . to beg.

The man said nothing but looked at Alisdair with grave, brown eyes that were sunken in deep hollows. The face itself was camouflaged with grime and wrinkles. There was a matted beard. The head was covered by a yellow beret. This was kept in place by a scarf which was tied over the top and round his neck to protect the man's ears from the cold – or perhaps from unwanted sound?

Alisdair stood and waited, prepared to give alms for the love of . . . for the love . . . of . . . for the love of himself. That was the truth of it, but the eyes looked out and still, no sound. He sat there and Alisdair noted his dress, as though he were looking in a man's outfitter's shop window. The man wore layer upon layer of coats and overcoats tied up with string and neckties. As he looked at Alisdair his fingers crept about the newspapers and cardboard in octopus-like fashion. Feeling? Searching? At the moment that Alisdair turned to leave, the voice spoke.

'Would you have a cigarette?'

Relieved by this simple request Alisdair took out two from his packet . . . and then sought his pocket for a pound coin. The man accepted the cigarettes but when Alisdair proffered the coin he shook his head. 'No, it's just the cigarette.'

Alisdair persisted and thrust the coin forward and spoke, and spoke out. 'I'm from Glasgow. I'm from Glasgow too. Take it . . . take it.' The man lowered his eyes from Alisdair's gaze. His fingers trailed over Alisdair's palm and took the money. He did not look up again and Alisdair walked on. He felt no superiority because of his pity. This was probably a good thing as pity always elevates the perpetrator of it – but compassion shares in the suffering. Strange how the greater of these two qualities seemed to emerge more in his private life than his professional one.

He started his car engine. He would see Veronica a little earlier than he had planned. He felt genuinely sorry for her. He did not like Veronica, but she did run a very good home – far better than most of the ghastly private ones that he had visited, some of which had verged on horror. Veronica *did* work extremely hard. He would offer her support at this time. He burped, then began his journey with a professional sigh.

Veronica had peeled off her dove-grey tights (such an attractive shade), lifted her navy blue skirt to just below her dimpled thighs and had just placed her feet in a bowl of hot water that immediately offered comfort to her aching feet. The water-softening salts had changed its hue to bright green, so that now she could not see that her feet were joined to her not unattractive ankles. Even this gave some pleasure as it made her two, normally painful corns both invisible and painless.

There was a tap at the door. Veronica had been expecting one of her ancillaries to bring her a cup of tea. The woman's dog-like devotion and admiration often irritated Veronica – and it was with a sharp tone that she called: 'Come in. Come in.'

Within ten minutes, therefore, Veronica had received a double shock – it was not the minion who entered but Alisdair McClennon.

'I'm sorry about being so early. I really didn't want to come upon you unawares . . .' He turned quickly to close the door behind him giving Veronica time to adjust her skirt a little below her knees. 'No, no, don't get up. I do the same myself. Corns, is it? I have corns that reseed themselves on both of my little toes –

at least twice or three times a year they seem to do it.' He talked in this amiable way as he made his way to the chair behind her desk. He spoke in a familiar tone as though they had been sharing the room for some time, or perhaps even, even living together.

Veronica moved her feet around in the bowl of water. She was aware that her tights were draped over the arm of her chair. Alisdair McClennon did not appear to notice them but shocked her again. 'I can fully understand your upset about this report, Veronica. We shouldn't let Mr Nigel Gosling . . . What's 'is name? Gobling . . . get away with it.'

Another deeper shock (had she been prone to it) might have brought a blush to her cheek. Veronica! Veronica! He had never ever used her Christian name before and his slight Scots accent gave an extra verve to the 'V'. Her name had never sounded so good. It had to be the warm water that made not just her feet and ankles suffused with warmth but the whole region of her legs and thighs. There was a tap at the door. 'Could you bring two cups, dear,' Veronica called out sharply. The moment was too precious for interruption.

'It's so kind of you to come along . . . Alisdair . . . Mr Gobling has informed me that his wife Daphne is coming along with his party of children, too. And that she, if you please, will choose the winners of the competition. "We will organise and do everything," he said. "You just take a back seat". It's the bloody patronage that makes me feel so angry and hurt and d. . .'

'But we all do it. It is a human frailty that comes with power. We all do it.' Alisdair cut in gently and seemed not too pre-occupied with what he was saying.

'Do what, Alisdair?' Veronica felt her breast tightening and swallowed hard.

'Patronise. After a time, we do it without realising it. It can get out of hand. In the insane it is referred to as delusions of grandeur. An amusing form of madness, I think; he does, however, need controlling – or should I put it more kindly – modifying.'

'And how should we modify Mr Nigel Gobling and his wife

Daphne? You tell me, Alisdair. You seem to know quite a bit about it.'

'Simple. I think we should do exactly as he expects. We should take a back seat. Presumably, he is well-versed in all the management problems concerned with the elderly so we need not be concerned about anything untoward happening.'

For response a deep chuckle seemed to emerge from the depths of Veronica's stomach. Eventually a volcanic eruption of laughter burst through the room and spread to Alisdair. The ancillary, lips pursed, placed the tray on the desk and left the room quickly. Surely, people in their positions shouldn't behave in such a frivolous way. She could still hear the laughter and the cackling some yards down the corridor.

Between chuckles Alisdair managed to say: 'Mr Checket's and Mrs Thurston's wedding should make good newspaper copy for you – had you considered yourself in a photograph with the happy pair? A nice opening for the New Year, don't you think?'

How clever, how very clever this apish looking man was, Veronica thought.

'I would like to be a witness at the wedding after all, Alisdair. I have come to be fond of Peggy and Henry. There is something about them, something that I can't quite place my finger on, something that I admire. I think . . . I think it is their integrity. Not in words, or in statements, but in being.'

'Perhaps we will all attain it one day. At least, if we don't it will come upon us with death.' The last word he spoke seemed to jolt Alisdair's memory. 'Ah, there is something I think I should tell you. I have applied for early retirement. If all goes well, then, I shall leave my duties behind at the end of March next year.'

Veronica looked wistful, 'We shall miss you. I shall miss you, Alisdair.' Veronica spoke fondly as though she were saying farewell to someone she had met all too briefly on a holiday romance.

'Oh, I shall call in and see you, on an informal basis, as a friend.'

'Does that mean that you won't ever give me any advice?'

'I would only advise if you asked, Veronica.'

Veronica brushed a permed curl away from her left eye. The steam from the bowl had caused it to be unreasonable. 'Just one request, a simple one, before we drink our tea. We don't want to let it get cold.'

'Yes?'

'The towel.' Veronica raised her right arm and pointed towards Alisdair's pelvic region. 'The towel – it's hanging over the back of the chair you're sitting on. Could you bring it over to me?'

'Of course, of course, how foolish of me.' She caught the trace of embarrassment in his voice, noticed his flushed brow and cheeks.

Veronica made no attempt to take the towel from his hand. She let him kneel down before her. He spread it on the floor. His face was within a few inches of her feet. He gazed up at her from this position.

'Shall we take our tea now?' she asked. 'It seems we have something in common.'

'What?' he asked as he watched her place one foot then another on the towel. 'Hard skin,' she replied.

CHAPTER
15

___

'She must have been a big woman, Peggy. Your friend, Miss Lamb, must have been very big for a lady, and if you don't mind me saying so, her clothes aren't at all usual, at least they're not what you'd expect a vicar's daughter to wear.' Henry spoke as he hauled himself into a huge pair of bottle-green knickers which were elasticated just below his knees.

Peggy ignored his observations, her mind set on the creative task she had set herself. 'Wear this pullover' she said. 'Miss Lamb was fond of it. It's a nice shade of brown. Hand knitted she said it was.'

Henry found that the pullover was as loose fitting as the knickers and Peggy continued approvingly. 'Oh, it looks lovely, Henry, and the yellow stags round the bottom of it give it a woodland-like look.'

'I didn't think stags were yellow, Peggy.'

'They're not, Henry, they're brown, but if you had brown stags on a brown pullover you wouldn't see the stags would you? I hope you're not going to start whining now we've got this far.'

'Sorry, Peggy, I don't want to let us down. It is hard, though, dressing up as someone very young if you are very old. I mean, in a way, it seems against nature.' Henry looked down at the brogue shoes and thick woollen stockings that had only ever been worn by Miss Lamb and himself as he spoke.

'Nature is kinder that that, Henry. It gives room for differences. Sometimes I feel about twelve, and I might say, you sometimes act as though you were bloody well seven. Well, we are going down there as the "Babes in the Wood". Quite honestly, we look a right sight from the outside, but I don't give a bugger about that. It's how we feel inside that counts.' Then, suddenly inspired, she cried. 'The holly – we can use it again. It brought us luck once. Pull some leaves off that sprig for me, but be careful not to prick yourself. Talking about pricks – did you know Mrs Oakley-Fenham is going as "The Sleeping Beauty"? If anyone kissed that old bat, they'd want to sleep for a hundred years if she woke up. Bend your head forward, Henry, I can stick some of these leaves into your woolly hat. Miss Lamb loved that hat. A drunken football fan gave it to her. It had a pom-pom on it but she cut it off. Said it was too fancy for her taste. Can you put a few leaves in my hair for me. They'll know we've been in a wood, then.'

Peggy's request was more difficult than it sounded as her hair was now reduced to the grey wisp here and there. Henry tried to be as delicate as possible but was rewarded with a shriek from Peggy.

'Ouch! Don't pierce my bloody scalp. Put most of them around the ribbon. Then they won't fall off. Shirley Temple wore a ribbon like this. Do you remember her, Henry? A little tap-dancing girl, she was – made a fortune wearing a ribbon and tap-dancing. It's all a dance, isn't it?'

'What is Peggy? I hope we won't have to dance.' Henry spoke with mournful, childish concern.

Peggy answered him soothingly. 'Now, now, now, we don't have to do anything that we don't want to do. You just sit here by me for a bit and settle yourself down.' She patted the space near her on the bed. She took his hand in hers and stroked it. 'There, now, there, there, we don't want to get upset, do we? We've both been upset enough in our time. There, there, there.' She continued stroking the back of his hand.

Although they looked grotesque, there might be those who could look further who may have smiled slowly at this vision of two children who had lost themselves in a wood far deeper than any of their imaginings.

———————

Alisdair stood at the lounge window and looked out on to the parking space next to the ornamental park. He wanted to see the visitors arrive. Arrivals were often indicative of what was to come, and Mr Gobling had said that he and his wife and party of eight children would arrive by minibus. Would they discuss anything outside? How would they usher the children from the minibus into the home? Would they give them a lecture on etiquette and good behaviour as they lined up on the gravel path? How much of an influence was Daphne Gobling on Nigel Gobling's aspiration? Observing an arrival as if one were a spy or a detective could give some answers.

A scent of countryside distracted him. He sniffed. A distinct smell of lavender – or could it be verbena? Quite close. It was at this point that he realised that Veronica had joined him. She stood as near to him as was possible without actually touching.

'You're watching out for them?' she asked.

Before he could answer the minibus came into view. They watched the vehicle disgorge its contents, noted what went on outside and then moved quickly from the window before either of them came into the view of their visitors.

'Daphne Gobling is in charge.' Veronica spoke with a flat, confident tone.

'I think you're right,' Alisdair muttered as the visiting party entered the lounge.

It was Daphne Gobling who led the group across the room. Veronica and Alisdair walked towards her as she led her husband forward. The pupils formed a semi-circle around the group of four adults. Daphne Gobling shook Veronica's hand firmly. 'Mrs Fairhurst?' Veronica nodded and smiled. Daphne continued, 'My husband, Nigel. He's portable, you know.' If this was a joke Veronica chose to ignore it. 'And you must be Mr Fairhurst,' Daphne ploughed on, 'I'm so glad that you have found time to come along, Mr Fairhurst.' She smiled widely to reveal a mouth full of large teeth. Veronica, thinking that if she had been blessed with teeth that size she would have been grateful for dentures, was able to smile before she spoke. 'This is Mr McClennon.' She touched Alisdair's shoulder. 'He is Director of Social Services in charge of the elderly throughout the borough. He is not portable. He came of his own volition.' Daphne tittered. 'I'm sorry. I'm so used to being side by side with my husband . . . It was foolish of me to presume . . .'

'No, not at all,' said Alisdair. 'Mrs Fairhurst and I were standing side by side – after all – but she is a colleague and friend. Not my wife.' All four laughed professionally, so ending the niceties of introduction.

Veronica surveyed the children who stood quietly awaiting a command from Mr Gobling. 'Do sit down, my dears,' Veronica cooed. The sight of the children had left her aghast. They had labels pinned to their costumes stating who they were and what they represented, and the costumes were so elaborate and so effective that all might have been cast in a horror film.

'Effective – don't you think?' Nigel Gobling's question was not asked for answering – it was the kind of self congratulation that the worst pedagogues often indulged in.

'Most,' was all Alisdair could say, as he looked at a girl dressed as an old witch of some fairy story. Why did the old and infirm have to be represented year after year in such a way? Another girl, dressed in a black jump-suit painted as a skeleton on the front and back was labelled 'Blithe Spirit'. As if this were not horror enough, next to her was a young boy resplendent in false, white beard and trailing smock holding a large wooden scythe, labelled 'Father Time'. Alisdair caught his breath and found himself quite involuntarily taking Veronica's hand. She felt his fear and his tension. 'They have even sent the "Grim Reaper" himself,' he whispered for her ears alone.

'We took the liberty of leaving our top clothes in the hall as we came in – if that is all right . . .' Daphne let the sentence fade as she wrongly assessed that her hosts were stunned with wonderment at the creative ensemble set before them.

'Yes, yes, of course, of course.' Veronica spoke quickly. She released Alisdair's hand and waved towards the assorted trays of food which had been placed on the coffee tables dotted about the room.

'Do let the children eat if they wish. I'm sure that they must like savouries.'

'Help yourselves, children,' Nigel Gobling called out. None of the children took up the offer. Most of them knew a stale kitchen leftover when they saw one.

'My party will begin to emerge soon.' Veronica looked at the expensive Japanese camera hanging from Nigel's neck. 'We have always tried to avoid labels, labels of any kind, so I'm afraid you will have to guess what characters they are from their costumes . . . and . . . er . . . er . . . their demeanour. They will make their way down the double staircase . . .' Veronica pointed towards it . . . and then glanced, disconcerted, at a child with numerous balloons floating from her legs, arms, head . . . everywhere . . . all about her. She was entitled 'An Old Gas Bag'.

Alisdair saw the fury in her eyes and now it was his turn to take her hand. 'Leave it. Say nothing,' he muttered.

'I'm afraid there are only four entrants from the residents here – originally we had eight but four have withdrawn – fatigue, you know.' Veronica's even tone changed as she caught sight of one of her residents teetering on the top landing of the stairway. 'Ah! Here's our first entrant.'

They watched a woman in a black chiffon negligee stretch out a thin, white arm and clutch the banister with a be-ringed hand. It was the kind of night-garment that might have graced the star of an American soap opera or possibly a soft-porn film. Mrs Oakley-Fenham's progress down the stairway was extremely slow. With one hand she trailed the banister whilst she stretched the other out before her. Every tortuous step brought her closer into view. The children had stopped chattering – they had never seen anything like this on television or video.

'Magnificent!' Alisdair responded in a stage whisper.

Mrs Oakley-Fenham had now stopped her progress. She paused at the foot of the stairs, eyes closed, arms outstretched. Her face was heavily made up as though she were some aged Coppelia – the long turkey-like neck decorated by folds and wrinkles was chopped in half by a string of choker pearls.

Most of those present had heard of people sleep-walking but it was something again to witness it. Arms still outstretched, Mrs Oakley-Fenham glided across the lounge. The whispers of awe, fear and concern from her onlookers gave her greater confidence with regard to the role that she had undertaken.

Alisdair watched as she floated herself down on to the settee, saw her raise one wiry old leg and then another before entering a state of repose. And there she lay her arms in a St Andrew's cross over her shrunken breasts. The eyes remained closed. A rattling, snorting kind of noise, apparently much too loud for the scraggy frame that sent it out, made Nigel Gobling jump up from his seat in alarm.

He appealed to Veronica. 'Is she all right? Is she all right? I hope the occasion hasn't proven too . . .'

'She is perfectly all right, Mr Gobling.' Veronica paused and smiled reassuringly. '"Perfect" is just the right word. Here is a new dimension to "Fancy Dress" and it is for you to enter it.'

'I'm sorry, Mrs Fairhurst, I don't know what you mean. I don't understand what you are trying to say.' Nigel Gobling sounded genuinely puzzled. Veronica laughed.

'I hadn't meant to talk in riddles, Mr Gobling. We are all limited by the extent of our experience.' She made a slight gesture with her hand toward Mrs Oakley-Fenham's recumbent rattling form. 'Here, here we have the "Sleeping Beauty" so much a part of the role, that she does indeed need awakening. I'm sure that we are all viewing the most realistic version of that most enchanting of stories. Are you going to be chivalrous for us all and play the prince?'

Nigel Gobling stood fixed like a traffic warden oppressed by vehicles on all sides. He turned to his wife who confirmed that he had to do what he dreaded doing. He knelt at the side of the sofa and bent towards the form, the face. He brushed the forehead with his lips. This desultory gesture had no effect whatsoever on a hundred years of slumber. The eyes remained firmly closed. He turned and looked towards his wife . . . she answered him by placing a forefinger to her lips.

It was necessary now for him to close his eyes in the face of duty as his lips touched the crimson gash. The audience gasped as reed-like, white arms coiled about his neck. After such a slumber a real kiss was required and Mrs Oakley-Fenham savoured the moment. She had not kissed like this since her days in the WRNS. After some seconds Nigel Gobling extricated himself and sat back on his knees. He did not feel capable of rising. Mrs Oakley-Fenham opened her eyes. Her smiling, beatific expression changed dramatically when she saw Nigel kneeling at her side. She yelled with exasperation. 'Oh, my God, it wasn't worth it. I wanted a real man.' She pointed towards Alisdair. 'I wanted him.'

Veronica spoke soothingly. Nigel Gobling somehow got himself back to the safe territory close to his wife. 'Never mind, dear, you're awake now and the choice is yours. You can choose your own prince. Ah,' Veronica pointed at the stairs, 'here is another one of our contestants.' Veronica knew from her various experiences of working with politicians that diversion was one of the best forms of control.

Daphne Gobling looked toward the stairway. Yet another person, this time a man, was making his way down the staircase. Were they all obsessed with bed-time? At least this one was well covered. He wore a nightcap, a nightshirt and carried a candle holder with an unlit candle stuck in it. 'How nice. It's Wee Willie Winkie,' she declared, as though she were making the discovery of the universe.

'How clever of you, my dear. You are quite right, of course. Our Mr Harding is still as sprightly now at eighty-two as he was when he was sixteen.' Veronica considered her own words. This was more truthful than she would care to admit, as Mr Harding had something of a reputation for bottom pinching and similar adolescent ploys which gave no thrill to anyone but himself. In his manhood, he had been a well-known rugby player, a man's man, who had women but never liked them. He had remained perplexed as to why both of his wives had divorced him. Nevertheless, he joined the throng in a buoyant spirit; Daphne and Nigel muttered in agreement that he seemed a jolly, decent, kind old fellow.

A cacophonous bubbling and giggling suddenly erupted from the children. Its cause stood at the top of the stairs. Henry and Peggy stood hand in hand oblivious to this premature reception which no one could have described as kind. 'Shush! Shush!' Veronica silenced the institutionalised brood. She felt Alisdair grip on to her arm, glanced to see the tears he sought to control. Her being was filled with an enormous pride. 'They look wonderful, Alisdair! Wonderful! Our children – how brave. What dignity. Hold up your head, Alisdair. That's it.' Veronica commanded him and made her way to the foot of the stairway.

'Henry! Peggy!' she called out to them as though she had recovered a deep friendship, a deep love from the past which she had long since thought lost forever. 'My babes in the wood . . . This is the way out. Down here . . . down here. This is the way.' She held out her arms in maternal fashion – something that was quite new to her. For the first time Peggy and Henry came towards her willingly.

Alisdair pondered over the scene before him. It was doubtful whether this incongruous pair would win first prize. Originality never received its due, but if the award were for valour or gallantry then, surely, Peggy and Henry should have it. To Veronica their appearance was not comic, it was appealing and moving. Their weird visual statement had cut Daphne and Nigel Gobling's patronage to the bone. It had slashed away their veneer of kindness to reveal their disapproval – as far as the Goblings were concerned the aged and ugly should be hidden away.

'Peggy Thurston and Henry Checket as the "Babes in the Wood".' Veronica announced her residents' arrival on the scene as if they had already won an academy award. Alisdair clapped loudly and the Goblings' dutiful children emerged from a state of mirthful paralysis to join him. Peggy and Henry left the stairs and followed Veronica. Henry sat in the chair that Veronica had vacated and with the utmost courtesy Alisdair offered Peggy his own. Peggy saw Veronica slide her arm through Alisdair's as they stood near.

Then Daphne Gobling began to orchestrate events.

'Before we judge the Fancy Dress we have a treat for you all.'

'A treat?' Peggy had become addicted to chocolate and her question was tinged with hope.

'Yes, my dear. We are having party games.'

'Oh, my God, I hate them,' Mrs Oakley-Fenham intoned.

Daphne Gobling wagged a finger in an expression of jaunty correction – 'Ah! But there are prizes for the winners.'

'Good!' Peggy declared. The thought of chocolates once again dissolving into her mouth caused her to lick her false teeth vigorously, making a clicking noise.

'Did you want us to help with the . . .' Veronica could get no further.

'No, no, no. You go off. This is a rest time for you – Adrian and I will hold the fort here for the next hour or so. Do let your helpers know that we will not need assistance.' She shooed Veronica away as though she were an interfering pigeon.

'But . . .' Veronica got no further with her remonstration. Alisdair began to lead her gently from the lounge.

'Let her hold the bloody fort. Remember what happened to General Custer,' he muttered to Veronica, and then called out over his shoulder. 'It's all in your capable hands, Mr Gobling.' Veronica glanced back once before turning into the corridor.

'Some sherry, Alisdair?'

'That would be nice . . .'

'Surely you haven't gone teetotal.'

'Oh, no, it's just that your sherry glasses are a wee bit small.' He took a breath and added, 'In fact they are absurdly small.'

'In that case, we will find something more suitable for you.'

'For us both.'

'Surely. For us both,' Veronica agreed.

CHAPTER
16

———————

Anyone watching Daphne and Nigel Gobling would have realised that order and inculcation was assuredly part of the curriculum in their scheme of things – after all it was so much simpler than the sort of discipline and education that always spewed up more questions than answers.

It had taken only a few minutes to arrange the chairs in orderly rows, and less than that to organise the seating; the old sat next to the old and the young sat next to the young.

Nigel Gobling had pinned a large outline of a donkey against the french windows blocking the view onto the lawn. He clapped his hands merely for attention, as the would-be revellers were already silent. He smiled and pointed to the donkey. Peggy began to wonder if something had happened to him as he stood there like some tailor's dummy. The click of his wife's camera released him from his pose and he spoke to Peggy. His training had taught him to remember names.

'Mrs Thurston, I'm sure that you can tell us the answer to his question.' Henry nudged Peggy who seemed to want to get through the proceedings by way of a little snooze. 'Tell us, Mrs Thurston, tell us, tell us which lady rode on a donkey at Christmas time?'

Peggy wondered if the man had gone out of his senses – rode on a donkey in the cold? With all the traffic about? She answered quite calmly. 'Somebody who'd gone off their rocker, I would think.'

The answer was quickly provided by a pious child in the front row. Nigel thought that it would be advantageous to begin the game as soon as possible. One question would set the ball rolling – it would be quite impossible to get the answer to this one wrong.

'Now, Mr Checket . . . I wonder if you would do something for me?'

'Well, I will if I can,' Henry replied obligingly.

'I'd like you to look at this drawing very, very carefully. It's a drawing of a donkey, isn't it?'

'Yes, it is. It couldn't be anything else,' said Henry.

'Ah, but tell me what is missing from the drawing. What has the artist (who happens to be my good wife) forgotten to give the donkey? His ears? Nose? Neck? Legs? Well, they are all there. What has my wife missed out?'

Henry stared at the drawing. He'd seen donkeys on the beach at Blackpool. The drawing seemed to correspond well enough with what he remembered of them. He scratched his bald patch, and rubbed his brow. He could see nothing missing. The animal appeared to be complete. It wasn't a freak.

'Perhaps this will give you a clue.' Adrian waved a strip of paper some fourteen inches long backward and forward in pendulum-like fashion in front of him. Henry felt none the wiser and decided to confer with Peggy.

She cupped her hand to Henry's ear and whispered, 'It's his prick.'

'Oh! Oh! How rude!' Henry exclaimed, 'What a thing to ask in front of children. I honestly don't think that you should have . . .'

'It's the donkey's tail, Mr Checket. It's his tail.' Adrian placed it in its correct position. 'It goes here.' He wasted no more time and quickly explained the rudiments of the game.

The aged within the company would have opted out except that there was a promise of a prize, and prizes for the elderly were few. Any bouquet that they might expect to receive would probably grace their coffins. It was a bonus to receive something whilst they were still alive.

This expectation of some kind of reward did not cast away the doubts and fears that the prospect of being blindfolded held for them. The children had easily acquiesced to the scarf being tied about their eyes and had pinned the wretched tail somewhere on or near the donkey. When Henry's turn came, he called in fear. 'Take it off! Take it off!' He had seen men shot dead in this way and had let the memory of it go. Now, unmercifully, he was reminded.

'He doesn't want to play. He doesn't have to, does he?' Peggy had got herself to his side and unknotted the scarf from behind his head. She held it in her hand. 'It's my turn. I'm the last. You sit down, Henry.'

'Not tight, not tight,' she said to Daphne Gobling, 'don't tie it tight. I've got a glass eye, dear, and it will pop out if you tie it tight.' Daphne Gobling, horrified, was happy to let Peggy adjust her own blindfold.

Like most avid competitors Peggy felt no qualms of guilt about lying or cheating. In the present circumstances it seemed the only sensible thing to do. In her crab-like mode of movement she made her way directly towards the outline of the donkey and paused before it. Some of the previous competitors had also cheated and there were at least three crosses very near where the tail should be. Peggy decided on brazen action and implanted the amputation at its precise growth point. There were some murmurs of disapproval, some questionings of Peggy's integrity from some of the bolder children. These mutterings of discontent were quickly silenced by Nigel Gobling as with the utmost gentleness he removed the scarf from Peggy's head.

'Oh, I've won!' she exclaimed and then turned to Henry. 'We've won, Henry.' Henry did not feel embarrassed that his applause was solitary.

'And here is your prize, Mrs Thurston.' Daphne Gobling advance smilingly to Peggy's side, 'but close your eyes and hold out your hands for a lovely surprise.' This time, Peggy did not cheat. She extended both palms and closed both eyes. 'Open now. Open now,' Daphne Gobling chirped like an exultant blackbird.

The expression of disdain and contempt which toured the

contours of Peggy's face gave Daphne some cause for concern. The laughter from the children faded as quickly as it had begun. Peggy stared first at the carrot and then at Daphne and then at the carrot again. She gripped it in her right hand and then, with a quick movement which surprised the onlookers, flung it at Nigel. It struck him on the shoulder and as it bounced to the floor he bent to retrieve it.

'Give it to the harvest festival,' Peggy snapped as she sat down – the timing of church seasons had never meant much to her and the carrot held no appeal for her mercurial teeth or hardened gums.

Nigel shoved the carrot quickly into his jacket pocket. He would curtail the evening. There would be only one more game, not three. The fancy dress would be adjudged afterwards. 'When in any doubt – play safe,' he thought. Something sedentary, something that required little ... 'Our last game, then.' He announced this as though what had gone before had been hugely entertaining. 'Now it's "Pass the Parcel". All the chairs in a ring, please.' The setting was changed as swiftly as a mammoth RSC theatre production.

Daphne Gobling started the tape on her recorder. The selection was from the Swingle Singers. The scat noises emitted puzzled both Henry and Peggy as the words did not seem to make much sense. The parcel went round and round. On receiving it, Peggy flung it to the child next to her as though it had burned her fingers. She was not interested in being surprised a second time.

Music stopped, music started, wrapper after wrapper fell on to the carpet.

'I have to congratulate you. I have never before tasted tea that held the satisfaction and pleasure of this particular brew.' As if to give proof of his observation, Alisdair drank again from the cup.

'It's fun drinking sherry this way. And it even looks like tea. I never take milk in mine, anyway.' Veronica felt unusually relaxed and let her left arm flop down the side of her armchair. Alisdair followed the line from her shoulder to her elbow, wrist, and fingers. Lying on the floor just inches from her finger tips was a rather battered-looking doll, its limbs awkwardly displayed as though in spasm. It looked quadriplegic and because it looked so different, it held Alisdair's gaze.

Her head resting on the high-backed chair, Veronica was unaware of Alisdair's distraction; with eyes half-closed she mused her thoughts.

'I was thinking, Alisdair – I was thinking about a small change in accommodation arrangements.' His lack of verbal response she took as an invitation to present her case. 'As you know, there are two flats here. One is for myself when I am on night call and the other is for one or the other of my two deputies when they are on rota. For the past year, the deputy posts have always been filled by agency posting. I'm sure the agency staff would be just as happy with a bedroom. Of course, a small Belling cooker and electric kettle could be provided. There would be no loss of comfort for the staff.'

'And the vacated flat?'

'I thought Peggy and Henry might like to move into it. It is next to mine – and for some reason I feel the need to be close to them.'

'What a good idea. It would also give you space for an extra resident. The waiting list is very long.'

'Do I have your informal permission?'

'You have it formally. I'll put it in writing tomorrow, Veronica, my dear.'

At this small term of endearment, Veronica looked up. Alisdair was staring down at the carpet beside her. 'Oh, you've discovered Nancy.' Veronica picked the doll up from the floor and held it by its head. It seemed as though some time-switch connected the movement with a set speech that went off in her head.

'I have her near me because she brings back happy memories of when I was a girl – she reminds me of my mother, brings her most forcefully into view. My mother was a widow left to bring up two young children. We kept a newsagent's shop in Tottenham – there was a better class of person living there then and . . .' Quite suddenly, Veronica gave a strangled, anguished cry, dropped the doll back on to the floor. She buried her face in the palms of her hands and began to sob.

She felt Alisdair's comforting arm about her shoulders and did nothing to check her weeping. Between the tears and the short intakes of breath words tippled forth. 'It's lies . . . all rubbish . . . never knew my father . . . nor my mother . . . wasn't really born . . . just happened . . . a war orphan . . . a woman I called Aunty . . . she said my mother had been just a child when I was born . . . taken from her . . . was I a product of incest? . . . at the end of the war . . . sent with hundreds of other orphans to Australia . . . came back here when I was twenty-one.' Veronica curbed her weeping and looked sorrowfully into Alisdair's eyes. 'You see, I don't know who I am. I would have liked to have had parents. I didn't have them, so I invented them.'

Alisdair patted her shoulder and said, 'You might not have liked them.'

Veronica shook her head slowly and sadly. 'Perhaps. Yes, I suppose you're right.' She smiled and added, 'Now I don't even like the ones that I have invented.'

'But you can let them go,' said Alisdair. 'They have ceased to exist.' He allowed his arm to continue to rest about her shoulders.

―――――――――――

Mrs Oakley-Fenham no longer felt like playing her role. That part of her that was still a sleeping beauty longed for slumber. She could barely keep her eyes open and the present course of activities caused her irritation to increase beyond its usual peak.

She had received a parcel, a gift, only to have it snatched from her hands by the wretched girl with helium balloons all about her. Five times this had happened and Mrs Oakley-Fenham was furious that such gross behaviour and bad manners in a child should remain unchecked. What did they teach children nowadays?

Again she received the parcel, but this time she held it clamped in her bony fingers. The child began to tug at it with small, grasping, podgy hands and strength was beginning to win against experience when Mrs Oakley-Fenham delivered a sharp slap, a well directed blow across the cheek of the youthful miscreant.

Hearing the wailing and howling noises emanating from the lounge, Veronica and Alisdair drained their tea cups and hastened to the scene of distress. They were welcomed by Nigel as though they had just arrived to rescue him from a desert island.

'Ah, you're just in time, Mrs Fairhurst. The games are over, now. We've had such fun, such a splendid time. Haven't we, children?' Little more than a murmur greeted this question which took more the form of an appeal.

Veronica noted that Daphne Gobling was comforting an overweight child garlanded with ringlets, ribbon and helium balloons. So this was the source of the wailing, now reduced to the odd whine and snivel. Even these last judderings of grievance came to a halt as Daphne delivered some piece of information which produced a valiant grin. Veronica doubted whether she had ever seen such a miserable looking group of revellers. They sat like people who had just been told to make yet another dental appointment.

'And now, I'm going to announce the winner of the Fancy Dress Competition.' Nigel paused in order to give the gathering some drama or tension that is sorely lacked. 'It was very close. My lady-wife and I found it very difficult to decide.'

'Why can't the bloody fool get on with it,' Alisdair rasped.

'The winner is . . . the winner is . . . Margaret Mathews, here today as "The Old Gas Bag".' He waited for the murmurs of approval and applause which never came and then he went quickly on with his preamble.

'Runner-up is Mr Harding for his original version of "Wee Willie Winkie" and the third is . . .'

Nigel's statement faltered as Mrs Oakley-Fenham glided gracefully past him. She was immediately followed by Peggy and Henry. They were not interested in the prospect of a bronze medal. 'Not worth staying, Henry, not worth it. Not worth any effort. I only got a carrot for a first. God knows what they might give us for a consolation. Bar of scrubbing soap, or a packet of soda crystals . . . Not worth staying.' Peggy's audible exit pronouncements had a deadening effect even upon Nigel, and he was now anxious to see this event reach a quick conclusion.

Alisdair noticed that neither of the prize-winners had bothered to open their beautifully decorated gift packets. He couldn't blame them for lack of interest. He had always felt that elaborate covering was often the way of camouflaging a mean gift. It was highly possible that the coverings in this case were worth more than what they hid. The mystery held little interest for him. In any event, he was quickly called to activity by Nigel.

'I wonder if you would do us the honours, Mr McClennon?' He thrust an expensive looking camera into Alisdair's hands. 'Just a couple of photographs – something for my wife and I to remember the occasion by. I'm afraid we are both a little sentimental about such things. You're familiar with this type of camera?' Nigel was about to educate Alisdair but was ordered gruffly away.

'My own is identical to this one. Do make up your group.'

This was done with a rapidity that suggested premeditated planning. From left to right – Daphne Gobling (standing), Wee Willie Winkie (sitting), the Old Gas Bag (sitting), Nigel Gobling (standing). Alisdair adjusted the lens and focused the group – then waited. Surely, they were going to invite Veronica Fairhurst to join them . . . No, they were not. Yet another press picture to add to the curriculum vitae of Mr Gobling's career.

'Are you all ready?' Alisdair asked.

'No, just one moment. Not quite,' Daphne Gobling interjected. Alisdair felt relieved. They were not so grossly mean-minded as he had thought. 'I'd just like to add a touch of authenticity to the picture.' She took a tiny cigarette lighter from her handbag and with one swift click and snap she had lit Wee Willie Winkie's candle. 'There! It should look lovely. We are ready when you are.'

Whilst Alisdair looked into his camera, Wee Willie Winkie reverted to Mr Harding and looked at Daphne Gobling's buttocks. Like the haunches of some prize mare they looked ripe for a pat. This immature side of his character had remained with him from early manhood to old age. It was irremedial as it had been tolerated – even approved of in a jocular way – throughout most of his life.

As Alisdair pressed the switch Mr Harding leaned sideways, his lighted candle moved accordingly. There was a loud explosion. Screams. Another explosion. Another. And yet another. Alisdair, stunned by the effect, let the camera crash to the floor. His initial, naive thought was that the thing had been detonated in some way and that he had executed the group whose image he had been asked to record.

The winner of the competition was now screaming in hysterical fashion. She howled with the fury that comes from fright rather than physical injury. Bits of string with balloon remnants trailed from her. Daphne Gobling had fallen to the ground. Her husband seemed to have lost his glasses, and Mr Harding sat and stared at the startled onlookers with a fixed, innocent smile.

Alisdair had never questioned Veronica's power of authority, but never had he seen it put to such fast and devastating effect. She kicked the camera which lay near her foot with true venom, so that it skidded across the carpet and crashed against the wall. Within seconds, she was holding the distressed child by the shoulders – she gave her a quick shake, 'Stop it! Stop that noise! Now!' Then after these orders had achieved the desired result she held the child in her arms for a moment. 'There, there. You're not hurt.' Alisdair could only marvel at Veronica's management skills as she proceeded to bring order out of chaos.

She retrieved Nigel's spectacles from behind one of the chairs and passed them to him without comment. She waited while

Daphne Gobling gradually hauled herself from the floor and tottered to her feet. Veronica offered her no comfort but said, 'Mrs Gobling – er – your dress.'

'Pardon me?' Daphne Gobling whimpered in a wavering manner.

'Your dress, Mrs Gobling. Your skirt. Would you kindly adjust it. There are children and men present here. Your suspenders are showing.'

It would be difficult (in an historic sense) to imagine a retreat more humiliating than that of the Goblings and their corps. In a circumspect way they had arrived to declare their superiority over the aged with a pretence at kindness simply to add to their own self-elevation. The vain-glorious now left the premises bedraggled and defeated.

Alisdair picked up the smashed camera and placed it on one of the coffee tables. He felt pervaded with a sense of optimism which was firmly grounded not in reality but in the face of extreme adversity.

Veronica surveyed the debris in the lounge and declared, 'I feel quite exhausted. I also feel curiously elated.'

'I can quite understand that you could feel both and I must admit that I share your state of being.'

'You'll stay and have another sherry before you leave us?'

'Gladly,' Alisdair replied as he marched behind Veronica towards her office.

CHAPTER

17

_____

Three days into the new year and even the view of devastation that met Veronica's eyes as she looked out on the grounds brought her little dismay and her state of inner well-being remained unsullied. For the past three days there had been raging gale-force winds that were said to have been unprecedented in their fury. This natural force now seemed to have exhausted itself but had left a legacy of damage behind in case anyone should forget too soon.

In the early morning light the landscape that Veronica surveyed looked as though it had received an air-raid from enemy bombers. What did they call it? Indiscriminate bombing? Veronica could not remember – but she could see that the gazebo was now flattened. Two of the large plane trees were fallen, lost forever, the lattice fencing smashed beyond repair, two of the benches upturned, and of the four trees left standing all seemed to have suffered terrible injuries. Great boughs had snapped and now hung loose, lurching in sickening fashion.

The day was cold and the sky grey but at least the wind had passed and Veronica was grateful of this as today was Henry and Peggy's wedding day. She had reminded them of this fact only last night but the information did not seem to register as vitally important. She was a shade disappointed by their lack of response. Perhaps she herself was somewhat to blame for this as she had acted just a little prematurely in organising their new living arrangements.

They now occupied the small flat next to her own. They had

been there for just over a fortnight. Few eyebrows had been raised when the move had been disclosed to the staff. 'Well, at their age it can only be for comfort and company, can't it?' one of her ancillaries had observed as she helped trundle the two single beds into the small bedroom. Henry had been delighted with his new quarters and Peggy had expressed satisfaction and had made only one moderate request and this was to do with the positioning of furniture. 'Could you push the two beds closer together? Just a small space between the two.' Veronica had failed to veil her surprise and Peggy had quickly added, 'Only I like to hear him breathing. He's always asleep before I am and the sound of his breathing soothes me. Otherwise I drink too much cocoa and . . . well, I hate piddling myself.'

Veronica thought about these things and marvelled that Peggy had diagnosed a cure for her intermittent bouts of enuresis. Since the move, her sheets had remained dry. This had surprised her, but on reflection, other changes had surprised her more. She had found that she did not call in on Henry and Peggy merely out of a sense of duty. She really enjoyed being with them and took enormous pleasure from their company.

This realisation shocked her. Her husband had not complained when more of her free time was spent at her institutional accommodation than either of her two homes. He was a kindly, subservient man whose needs could be met without much effort. Veronica was compassionate and she was not a fool. The country cottage was now up for sale. For some reason, she did not feel that she was the woman she had previously thought she was.

Thanks to Henry and Peggy, she was no longer referred to as 'Mrs Fairhurst'. It was now 'Veronica'. This familiarity had not lessened her authority or esteem within the home, but increased it. Somehow, it inferred that she was not just in charge of the home but a very part of it. Its inmates were not just residents but relatives.

Today (however bleak the meteorological outlook) heralded pleasure and excitement for Veronica. She had dressed carefully in a pinkish-mauve suit, and planned to wear a spray of orchids pinned to her lapel. She looked at the flowers which stood in some kind of green sponge that kept them alive and fresh.

When Veronica had discussed with Peggy the kind of bouquet that would be appropriate for a mature bride, Peggy had not been awkward or stubborn, but impossible.

'Well, I like railway flowers,' she had said in a non-commital way.

'Oh, Peggy, wouldn't you like tulips?' Veronica knew these flowers were imported and available in abundance at the florist shops.

'I've never seen tulips growing near the railway. I don't want tulips. They are crude.' Peggy had stated this as a fact.

'Oh, we don't want anything crude.' Henry loved sounding proper.

'All railway flowers are lovely.' Peggy had related her knowledge of them. 'There's willow herb that looks like pink cathedral spires, and poppies all bold and red. And most of all, I like harebells. Their stalks are so thin that you could thread them through the eye of a needle – and the flowers are the palest blue.' Peggy had gazed into Veronica's face with an expression of babyish melancholy, '. . . they are the colour of your eyes. Lovely they are.'

The sincerity of Peggy's compliment and the lack of artifice in its delivery left Veronica so moved that she was unable to reply for some time.

'I've seen daffodils growing along railway embankments, Peggy. What about daffodils? Do you like them?' Veronica ventured.

'Yes, I like them, but let them stay where they are. Let them be. I don't think flowers want to be picked. Anyway, I'll have my hands full hanging on to Henry. He's my "Lily of the Valley".' She had laughed and Veronica had joined in as her mirth was in no sense derisive.

Her feelings at the prospect of seeing Alisdair now verged on adolescent adoration. Her own youth had been traumatically menstrual and dreary. There had been no awakenings. It was strange to experience such a thing at fifty-two – so much easier to celebrate.

It was over a week since she had last seen him – but she had received a Christmas card from him. The card itself had not been remotely festive and Veronica could not understand what a line drawing of a zebra had to do with Christmas. But the message, written in appalling, childish scrawl had been enough – 'love, Alisdair.'

With these two words sounding in her head Veronica's hand sifted through the several buff envelopes on her desk as she waited. Her working correspondence never lessened and it had to be dealt with. She opened the one marked 'Urgent' first. She absorbed the contents of the letter quickly and then read it again very slowly and tortuously, as though some heavy opiate dulling her brain required her to struggle. At first the absurdity of the footnote at the bottom of the letter lingered in her mind. 'In accordance with his personal wishes, Mr McClennon will be buried by the Society of Friends. His only known relative, a sister, is a nun whose order is a closed one, and she will not be attending the memorial service. Time and date of the service will be sent to you as soon as arrangements have been verified.' The real import of the letter now thrust at her breast and frame as though it were intent on wounding her.

'We regret to inform you that at one a.m. on January 1 your colleague Mr Alisdair McClennon met with accidental death. A van carrying New Year revellers swerved from the road and crashed through the plate-glass window of the "Uldag Kebab and Steak House" where Mr McClennon was dining with friends. Mr McClennon and Mr Yusaf Turabi were killed instantly and a third member of the company is in hospital in a critical condition. The driver of the vehicle (who has superficial injuries) is being held in custody concerning charges on driving dangerously under the influence of drink.

'This is, indeed, sad news for all of us who knew Mr McClennon.

'He first joined us in 1974 after completing four years as

assistant director in a major city in his native Scotland. Before this Mr McClennon had . . .' Veronica did not want to have to glean through the jargon of a career; it was his life that she wanted more of, not his past. Entering a rage that she did nothing to control, she stabbed at the telephone digits with her forefinger.

The saccharine-voiced personnel officer answered her question. 'Yes, I'm afraid it's quite true, Mrs Fairhurst. A great shock to us all. Deeply sad.'

'Have they charged him with murder?' Veronica hissed.

'I beg your pardon?'

'You don't have to beg for anything. That swine of a driver, the one who drove the van. A New Year reveller is not what I would call him. Have they charged him with murder?' Veronica began to shout into the telephone.

'Look, I can hear that you are distressed by this news, Mrs Fairhurst. We all are. Why not come back to me on it in a couple of days. Let things settle. You know we all have to learn to accept such things. There was no response from Veronica and the personnel officer wondered if she had been overcome by grief or trauma. 'Are you there, Mrs Fairhurst? Are you there?' he enquired softly.

Just at the point when he had given up all hope of receiving an answer, Veronica spoke – her voice harsh and terrible in its controlled venom. 'I curse that driver. I curse him. I wish him dead.' This ended the conversation. Receivers were replaced.

It would have been easier to bear if she had been in a position to organise Alisdair's burial, but these rights were not hers. The business of death, undertakers, forms, certificates would have been a palliative. She had nothing to keep her busy, nothing to calm her . . . the wedding? It had to go on. It would take place. She would not let Henry or Peggy know the truth. Not yet. Perhaps later. Timing was so important in such matters. Veronica felt Peggy and Henry were not ready for such dire tidings. She pinned the hothouse plant, the orchid, onto the lapel of her costume. 'Alisdair has been called away to chair an urgent conference.' She rehearsed the words and almost came to believe them herself.

It was Friday. It was three-thirty p.m. and it was an off-duty day for Veronica. Rather than browse around Marks and Spencer or visit the hairdresser, she chose to spend the afternoon with her friends Mr and Mrs Henry Checket.

The legal stamp on Peggy and Henry's coupling had taken place a month previously at a local registry office. The proceedings, after an initial upset (Henry would persist in answering questions that were put to Peggy), had gone smoothly. They had been pronounced man and wife.

These two now sat near her. Their attention was enraptured by the playful antics of a tabby kitten which Veronica (against all rules of health and hygiene within her department) had placed in their care.

'She is a naughty little thing,' Henry observed. 'Look at her shake her tail in that way. She's got spirit that cat has – Spirit!'

'She is not a "she", Henry. She's a "he".' Peggy dipped her digestive biscuit into her tea. 'It's a tom cat.' Peggy's swift recognition of the gender made Veronica smile. Her experience and knowledge of such matters clearly went much deeper than her husband's.

'It was strange how he kept wandering into the house,' Veronica mused aloud. 'Every time we would put him outside and then within an hour or so he would find his way in. Again, it was as though he had filed his own application for admission.'

'Cats will always go where they are wanted,' said Peggy. 'I expect that dead one we gave to Mac was his dad, and . . .' Peggy let the sodden biscuit fall into her tea cup. 'We could call it Mac, couldn't we?'

Veronica knew there was more in this question than naming an animal; it was a time for telling, a time for confidences. Intent on stating all she knew, she spoke quickly without pause.

'I have something to tell you both. It is sad news. I hadn't wanted to pass it on to you so soon, but I can see that now is the time for it. It concerns your friend Alisdair McClennon. You must be puzzled as to why he has not visited us for some time. I'm afraid that he will never come to see us again . . .' Here, Veronica broke down and wept; the first tears in all these weeks coursed down her cheeks. She cleared her grief.

Peggy placed her arm about her and Henry patted the back of her hand. Unused to physical comfort of this kind Veronica felt enormous relief. 'He won't come back because he is too honourable – you see, he knew that I was a married woman and adultery would have been abhorrent to him. Yes, you both should know that Alisdair McClennon and I were involved in a great passion. We tried to resist it, but were swept on by forces that neither of us could ever have imagined. It was his sense of duty that made him take the job abroad. We shall never see him again, and I will never know another man like I knew him.'

Peggy began to stroke Veronica's hair. It really didn't matter whether or not what she was saying was true or false.

'Never mind, lovely, never mind,' Henry murmured soothingly, 'you've still got me and Peggy. You've still got us.'

'Yes, yes,' Peggy agreed, 'they may not be perfect but you've still got your mom and dad.'

Veronica now calm and adopted, took the tea cups from the tray and carried them to the sink and, like the dutiful daughter that she had become, emptied the slops down the drain.